WILLARD PRICE

VOLCANO ADVENTURE

Illustrated from drawings by Pat Marriott

RED FOX

VOLCANO ADVENTURE
A RED FOX BOOK 978 1782 95021 9

First published in Great Britain by Jonathan Cape, Ltd
An imprint of Random House Children's Publishers UK
A Random House Group Company

Jonathan Cape edition published 1956
Red Fox edition published 1993
This edition published 2013

1 3 5 7 9 10 8 6 4 2

The Random House Group Limited supports the Forest Stewardship Council®
(FSC®), the leading international forest-certification organisation. Our books
carrying the FSC label are printed on FSC®-certified paper. FSC is the only
forest-certification scheme supported by the leading environmental
organisations, including Greenpeace. Our paper procurement policy
can be found at www.randomhouse.co.uk/environment

Red Fox Books are published by Random House Children's Publishers UK,
61–63 Uxbridge Road, London W5 5SA

www.randomhousechildrens.co.uk
www.totallyrandombooks.co.uk
www.randomhouse.co.uk

Addresses for companies within The Random House Group Limited can be
found at: www.randomhouse.co.uk/offices.htm

THE RANDOM HOUSE GROUP Limited Reg. No. 954009

A CIP catalogue record for this book is available from the British Library.

Printed in the UK by CPI Group (UK) Ltd, Croydon, CR0 4YY

pioneer traveller himself – over a period of sixty years

he visited one hundred and forty-eight countries. Of course, he travelled at a time when the aeroplane was just being invented, when people communicated by letter or telegraph, and so he travelled by motor car, ship, horse, and even by elephant and camel – there were few places on Earth that he wouldn't visit. He had many wonderful adventures, some of which may very well be in the story that you are about to read . . .

We are so pleased that you are about to embark on an adventure with the wise Hal and the impulsive Roger, and we wish you luck as you search with them for unusual wildlife and great adventure.

The granddaughters of Willard Price:

Katharine Price
Susannah Price Haney
Rebecca Price Brooks

VOLCANO
ADVENTURE

Contents

Author's Note

The chief characters in this book are fictional, but the volcanic events described actually happened. A bell containing observers did descend 1,250 feet into the boiling crater of Mihara, the *Kaiyo Maru* was sunk by a submarine exposion, divers discovered Falcon Island fifty feet below the surface, Tin Can's thirty craters erupted so savagely that the entire population had to be removed, Mauna Loa has frequently sent rivers of lava to the sea, and Hilo was saved by bombing.

The author has personally visited all the scenes described. In his pursuit of information on the habits of volcanoes, he has climed Asama, Aso, Mihara, Kilauea, Mauna Loa, Paricutin and Vesuvius, and has flown over Popocatepetl, Pelée, Momotombo, Izalco, Misti, Stromboli, Etna, Uracas and Apo.

VOLCANO
ADVENTURE

1
Volcano in the Night

It was very dark. A heavy blanket of fog hid the stars. The fog was so thick that the three mountain climbers could hardly see each other even with the help of their electric torches.

The fog was cold, the wind was cold, every bone in Hal's body was cold. It was necessary to climb the volcano at night, for it would have been too hot a trip under the broiling sun. But Hal, shivering, thought he would almost rather be too hot than too cold. He had given his sweater to his younger brother, Roger, but he still had his trench coat and this he zipped up to the chin.

Roger puffed and panted along beside him. The boy was usually merry and mischievous, but after three hours of stiff climbing he had very little fun left in him.

'This old volcano must be as high as the moon,' he complained. 'Aren't we nearly at the top?'

'Afraid not,' Hal replied. 'We may be half way there.' Roger groaned.

'Save your breath, boys,' said the third member of the party, 'you'll need it. The hardest part is ahead.' And Dr Dan Adams, volcanologist, scrambled up the face of a cliff as easily as if it had been a flight of stairs.

Ignoring his own advice to save breath, he burst into song. The song rose over the shriek of the wind and the rumbling of the volcano.

Hal wished he wouldn't sing. There was something wild about it, something not quite right. Perhaps it was meant to be a cheerful song, but it made a chill run down Hal's spine. The night suddenly seemed full of strange, terrible faces swimming by in the flying fog.

'Snap out of it,' said Hal, but he said it only to himself.

He must keep a grip on his nerves. There was nothing the matter with the song. Why shouldn't the man sing if he wanted to?

It would sound all right in the daytime. Perhaps it was just weird because of the night, the fog, the screaming wind, the muttering mountain, the quaking of the earth beneath, the fall of ash and cinders upon steel helmets, the occasional flash of light far above when the crater threw up its column of fire . . . the unreality of the whole thing.

That must be why the song seemed so strange, more like the cry of a wild loon than the voice of a man.

The doctor was no wild loon. He was a sober scientist.

He was the American Museum's expert on volcanoes. He had studied volcanoes all over the world. He had gone down into the craters, analysed the gases, measured the lava flow, charted the eruptions, written learned reports.

Volcanoes to him were just figures and facts. He was cool, mathematical, scientific, a brilliant scholar.

Hal thought how lucky he and Roger were to be chosen as his assistants. They knew nothing about volcanoes – but they had powerful young bodies and they had already had a few months' experience on expeditions in the Amazon valley and among Pacific islands.* Now summer vacation was almost over and they would ordinarily have been thinking about getting back to school. But since they were both below the average age of their classes their father, John

---

* For the story of these experiences see the books *Amazon Adventure*, *South Sea Adventure* and *Underwater Adventure* by Willard Price.

Hunt, the famous naturalist and animal collector, had allowed them a year off from their studies to get a practical education on expeditions for him and his scientific friends.

So here they were, half way up an exploding Japanese volcano in the dead of night with a man singing like a wild loon.

Whang! A cinder the size of a hen's egg struck Hal's helmet and bounced away.

Luckily these cinders, which had been white-hot when thrown up by the volcano, were cold after they had fallen through a mile of chill fog. Hal almost wished they were hot.

The cold wind blew the damp fog straight through his clothes; he could wring the water out of his coat.

Now and then they climbed out of the fog into clear air. But their torches showed another fog bank above them and presently they were in it. So they climbed from cloud to cloud.

And all this time there was a nice warm fire nearby.

Inside the mountain. Hal put his hand on the ground. He could feel the warmth. A terrific fire with a temperature ten times the boiling point of water was burning under his feet while he shivered and shook with the cold. He couldn't wait to get to the edge of the crater where he could enjoy the heat from this gigantic furnace.

Suddenly the mountain shook itself like a wet dog and sent up a spout of flame.

Then a new shower of cinders fell. Falling on steel helmets they were harmless enough, but when they struck shoulders or backs they bruised the flesh. And one never knew when something bigger might fall. Mt Asama had been known to throw out rocks as big as motor cars.

That wasn't likely to happen just now. Asama was not in violent eruption. If she had been, they wouldn't be climbing her. She was just in one of her muttering moods.

That didn't mean that she was quite safe. In fact, only a few days earlier two climbers had been killed by a shower of rocks, and a month ago a man was trapped between two streams of lava and burned to death. Ashes and cinders were pouring down upon roofs twenty miles away and earthquakes had tumbled several houses in the nearby town of Karuizawa.

But this was not much compared with what Asama

could do when she really got angry. In one eruption she had buried forty-eight villages a hundred feet deep under a river of boiling lava. That is twice as deep as Pompeii was buried. But then, Asama is twice the height of Vesuvius and can be twice as violent.

Now she seemed to be slowly building up in preparation for another terrific eruption. It might come in a year, a month, a day. Who could tell?

If anybody could tell, a trained volcanologist could. Perhaps Dr Dan Adams could solve the mystery of Asama.

Suddenly Roger stopped dead in his tracks. 'Ghosts!' he cried.

Hal and the doctor stopped and looked at Roger. Was the kid cracking up? Both of them had some advice ready for him, but before they could speak Roger said:

'Up there,' and pointed up the steep slope.

They looked but could see nothing. The fog closed in around them like a gigantic mosquito net. It swept swiftly across the ground, not in a solid mass, but in ripples or shivers before the wind. The doctor's wild singing had stopped but the wind was singing just as wild a tune and the roar of the volcano, the flashes of fire, the rain of rocks, the atmosphere of suspense and danger, were hard on the nerves. The boy couldn't be blamed for beginning to imagine things.

'What's the matter with you blokes?' Roger said disrespectfully. 'Up there!'

They looked again. Now they saw what Roger's keen eyes had picked out in the fog. Far up the slope, three lights seemed to be doing a ghostly dance.

Were they fireballs from the volcano? Were they the glowing parts of a stream of lava that was sweeping down upon them and would soon bury them in its blazing depths?

'Evidently we're not alone on the mountain,' said the doctor. He cupped his hands around his mouth and yelled, 'Hello-o-o-o!'

The lights above stopped moving. The three climbers listened. But no human voice rose over the scream of the wind and roar of the volcano.

The doctor called again. This time there was an answering cry from above.

'Come on,' said the doctor, 'we're going to have company.' And they lost no time climbing up around the lava boulders and over slippery ash until they came to the three lights, which they found were held by three young Japanese climbers.

'*Komban wa*,' said the oldest of the three, and ran on in Japanese. Then, as his torch caught the faces of the newcomers, he said.

'Ah, I think you speak English. I too speak English. I teacher of English in Nagoya Middle School. These are two of our students, Kobo and Machida. They no speak good like me. My name Toguri.'

The doctor introduced himself and his two companions and everyone shook hands, all equally delighted to have company on the climb to the crater's mouth. Now the night and the mystery, the fog and the cold, the wailing wind and thundering mountain, did not seem quite so nerve-racking.

And what made Hal and Roger especially happy was that the doctor did not sing any more in that weird, bloodcurdling way of his but talked reasonably and cheerfully as the six climbed on up the shaking mountain.

2
Fog and Fire

The darkness was turning from black to grey. Day was coming. Presently there was enough light to see by and they could turn off their torches.

And what a dreary waste they saw! Great black blocks of lava, streams of ashes, not a tree, not a bush, not a blade of grass. The moon itself could not be any more bare and bald. This was a place where nothing dared to grow and it seemed as if man himself had no right to be here.

Only the fog was perfectly at home, rushing and rippling over the wet black rocks. It came in bursts and billows. One moment you could see twenty feet ahead, the next moment you could hardly see your hand before your face.

In the darkness and fog they had lost what little trail there had been. Now they simply blundered upward, slipping in the ashes, scratched by the sharp, glassy ridges of lava, clambering up cliffs like mountain goats, trying to keep their balance when the ground shook. Suddenly a violent quake made the rocks bounce. There was a sliding, ripping sound above them.

'Look out!' cried the doctor. 'Under this ledge – quick!'

The six huddled in the shallow cave under the projecting ledge as tons of rock, ash and cinder thundered down like a deadly waterfall within a few feet of their faces. While it passed their hiding place it completely blocked out the light. Then it rampaged down the mountainside, its roar becoming fainter and fainter as it was swallowed up in the fog.

'Stay where you are for a minute.' A few rocks that had been too slow to keep up with the avalanche now came tumbling down. Some of them were quite big enough to kill a man. When all seemed quiet again, the climb was resumed.

At last the ground began to level out and the six weary volcanologists found themselves upon what appeared to be the top of the mountain. But where was the crater?

This was no simple volcano. It did not rise to a point.

The top of the mountain consisted of mile upon mile of hilly country. Somewhere there was a crater.

But, without a trail to follow, who could tell where it might be? In clear weather the rising smoke could be seen. In this dense fog, the six explorers could only see each other.

It was bitterly cold, for they were now more than eight thousand feet above sea level. The sweeping fog seemed to go straight through them. They huddled behind a great rock and held a council of war. The great rock split the fog as if it had been a river and it rolled by on either side.

'We make fire,' said Toguri, trying to speak cheerfully.

He looked about for wood. There was not a twig, not a leaf, to be seen anywhere.

The six ransacked their pockets and brought out various small pieces of paper. When they were all put together they made a pile a few inches high. The doctor set it alight and they all warmed their hands over the tiny blaze. In less than five minutes it was out.

'I hungry,' said Toguri. 'You hungry?' He produced a small wooden box and opened it to reveal some fish and rice. 'We call this *bento*. You like?'

'Yes, indeed,' replied Dr Adams. 'And perhaps

you would like some of this.' And he produced a few chocolate bars. So they shared each other's small provisions.

Roger, dipping into the bento box, got hold of something that looked like a white worm. He held it up and examined it doubtfully.

'Octopus tentacle,' said the cheerful Toguri. 'Very good. You like?'

'I like,' said Roger, and gulped it down.

Only one of the six did not eat. That was Kobo. He sat on a block of lava a little apart from the rest. His face was pale and drawn and he seemed to be sunk in painful thought.

The doctor stood up. 'Now, Toguri-san, how are we going to find that crater?'

The teacher of English waved his hands and grinned.Nothing seemed to bother him.

'Perhaps we no find. I think we lost. Perhaps fog go away, then we find. Perhaps fog no go away. Many miles of hills on top of this mountain. Sometimes people wander about in the fog here for days. We just stay here. Nothing we can do.'

Dr Adams did not say what he thought. He thought that Toguri must be a pretty poor teacher of English,

and a pretty poor teacher of courage.

'I think there *is* something we can do,' he said.

'Somewhere there's a trail leading to that crater. If we can find the trail we're all right. Now, I have a plan. We'll make a human wheel. You, Toguri-san, stay here. We five will go out as far as we can still hear your shout. That won't be very far because this fog deadens sound – perhaps about five hundred yards. We'll leave Machida there, then go five hundred yards farther, then leave Kobo, and go on out, posting Roger, and then Hal, and I'll be at the end. That will make a line nearly a mile and a half long. Then, while Toguri-san stays here at the rock, the rest of the wheel will begin revolving clockwise. If that trail is within a mile and a half of this rock in any direction, we'll find it.'

'Isn't someone likely to get lost?' asked Hal.

'Not if each man keeps within call of the next man at all times. Let's start. Keep shouting, Toguri-san.'

While Toguri settled back against the rock, well satisfied with his part of the plan, the five struck out into the fog.

'*Yoi!*' shouted Toguri, in Japanese fashion. They went on. '*Yoi . . . yoi . . . yoi . . .*' The shout was becoming faint now as they stopped and left Machida, then went on.

So the men were posted, calling back and forth to each other, until the line ended with the doctor.

'March!' he shouted. The command was passed down the line, and the big wheel began to move. It had not made more than a quarter turn when the doctor shouted, 'Here it is. The trail. Join me here.'

The word was passed down the line and within twenty minutes all stood together on the trail. But which way to the crater?

They listened to the volcano's roar. Because of the fog, it seemed to come from all around them, and from beneath, and from above. 'I think it may be this way,' said the volcano man, and struck off along the trail, the others following.

Kobo brought up the rear. Hal, glancing back, saw that the young student's face was very sad and his eyes were cast down. He dragged his feet. You would have thought he was going to his own funeral. What was the matter with Kobo?

Hal dropped back beside him and tried to start a conversation. But he knew no Japanese and Kobo was too shy to attempt to use the little English he had learned. He gave Hal a sad smile and they trudged on in silence.

If Kobo seemed unhappy, Dr Dan seemed a little too happy. Hal had come to think of him as Dr Dan. 'Just call me Dan,' Dr Adams had told him. 'After all, I'm only about ten years older than you, and you're a bigger man than I am.'

It was true that Hal, though only in his late teens, was a mite taller than the doctor, broader of shoulder and more powerful of body. But the doctor was wiry and strong, and very clever, Hal thought. Hal felt he owed the scientist some respect and could not quite bring himself to address him as Dan, but compromised on Dr Dan.

A shower of stones fell but Dr Dan did not seem to notice them. With his head up he marched on so fast that the others had difficulty in keeping up with him. The roar of the volcano grew louder. The sun had risen but was unable to get through the fog. The fog was more dense than ever because evil gases and smoke had joined it. Toguri was choking and coughing.

But in spite of the fumes and the falling stones and the quaking of the ground and the increasing thunder of the monster, Dr Dan strode along boldly, almost too boldly – as if he were afraid to show fear. And again he broke into the wild song of the night. It sounded as weird by daylight as it had in the darkness.

Suddenly he came to an abrupt halt. 'We have arrived!' he cried.

The others came up beside him. A few feet ahead the ground dropped away to nothing. Great billows of smoke rose to mingle with the flying fog.

Their eyes could make out nothing but their ears told them that they were standing at the edge of the crater.

3
Crater's Edge

A noise like the roar of ten thousand angry lions came up from the pit.

Beneath that noise there was another like the rumble of freight trains over a bridge. Then there was a higher note, the sound of escaping steam, like the hiss of a great serpent. And there were sudden explosions as if charges of dynamite were being set off.

The din became so terrific that when Dr Dan spoke again no one could hear him.

Hal remembered what he had read in *Terry's Guide*: 'Mt Asama is the largest, angriest and most treacherous volcano in Japan. The dangers at the summit are manifold and should not be regarded lightly.'

It was terrifying – and yet pleasant, because the heat rising from the fires beneath felt very good after a night in the chill fog. Each one of the visitors revolved like a chicken on a spit in order to warm himself all over.

From a bag that Hal carried, Dr Dan produced

various instruments, a thermometer, a pyroscope, a small spectroscope. He began to take readings and jot down the results in his notebook. He captured some of the rising gas in a test tube and put it away for later study.

He spoke again, but although the boys could see his lips move they could not hear a word. Dr Dan signalled to the boys to follow him and set off along the edge of the crater.

Hal, looking back, saw a strange sight. The three Japanese had lined up in a row and were bowing deeply to the smoking crater.

Hal had read about this – the way the Japanese worship their volcanoes. Their religion, Shinto, makes every volcano a shrine or holy place. The god of the volcano must be treated with deep respect or he will become angry and destroy the villages in the country below.

The god is a terrible god and nothing pleases him so much as human sacrifice. In the old days human victims were thrown into his hungry mouth. Anyone selected to be given to the god was supposed to regard it as an honour.

Nowadays no one is thrown to the god, but many

persons still give themselves to him of their own free will. In this way they think they are performing a holy act, and at the same time they are escaping their own troubles. The man who has lost his job may jump into a volcano. The woman whose children misbehave may end her life in the crater.

The young lovers whose parents will not let them marry may leap together into the flames. The student who has failed in his examination may choose to die here.

In Europe and America such an escape from duty would be considered cowardly. The Japanese do not think of it in that way and every year hundreds of disappointed people go to the arms of the fire god in any of the fifty-eight active volcanoes of Japan.

Hal looked back again. Toguri and Machida were wandering off along the edge of the pit. But Kobo still stood where he had been, gazing into the crater. Then he sat down on a rock and buried his head in his hand.

Hal wanted to go back to him. But what could he do? Perhaps there was nothing wrong. If there was, Kobo's Japanese friends could look after him. Dr Dan was already fifty feet ahead and signalling impatiently for Hal to come along. Hal hurried to catch up.

It was an exciting walk along the crater's edge. One side of your body was chilled by the fog, the other side baked by the fire-breathing monster. The ground was very hot underfoot. Hal found himself walking on the edges of his shoes to avoid the heat.

Here and there steam spurted up between the rocks. If you didn't watch where you were stepping and one of these steam jets shot up inside your trousers it was like being boiled alive.

The falling stones had been cold far down the mountainside. Here they were hot, and if one fell on your shoulder and stayed there for a moment it burned the cloth. Every boy likes to throw stones down a precipice. When Roger picked up a pebble to throw into the volcano he dropped it with a howl and sucked a burned hand.

The doctor was making a topographical survey of the crater's edge. Every hump and hollow, every fissure and steam jet, was carefully examined. Figures and facts went down in the notebook.

The noise was ear-splitting. Compared with that uproar, a steel mill would be as quiet as a cemetery. The fire god was gritting and grinding his teeth, then spitting them out in sky-rockets that flamed up through the gloom to a great height, changed as they fell from whitehot to red-hot, and slapped down on the rocks. There they lay, pasty plops of liquid rock slowly congealing into a sort of dough, still glaring red, and sending out a terrific heat.

The doctor rushed over to one and took a reading with his electric pyrometer. He showed the reading to the boys, 1100 degrees Centigrade.

Dr Dan shook his head gravely and pointed up. They understood his warning. These falling puddings were dangerous. They must keep watch above and not get struck by one of them. It was easy to imagine what would happen. One touch of this blazing lava, eleven times as hot as boiling, would set your clothes afire and you would go up in flame like a Roman candle.

But it was hard to watch both the sky and the ground at the same time. Roger got cross-eyed trying to do it. He wished he were a bird which can look in one direction with one eye and in the opposite direction with the other.

Suddenly the fog blew away and the sun lit up the dreary waste of grey ash and black lava and made a rainbow in the rising steam. The last ribbons of fog went up like writhing ghosts.

The volcano men stopped to look at the view. Thousands of feet below lay Japanese villages under thatched roofs, rice paddies like squares on a checkerboard, Shinto temples and pagodas on small hilltops, sparkling streams. Beyond the valleys rose ranges of mountains, blue in the distance. Far to the south was the perfect cone of Fuji. Away to the west gleamed the Japan Sea.

Splat! A blazing pudding of lava fell within ten feet of them. This was no time to be looking at the view and they went on warily, watching the sky and the ragged ground underfoot.

The gases made the eyes run with tears and irritated the nose and throat. Sometimes the fumes were suffocating and you just had to stop breathing for a moment and wait for the changeable wind to bring a gust of fresh air.

Then the breeze carried the gases away and pushed the column of smoke and fire to one side so that they could see down into the crater for the first time. The sight was terrible – and Hal, happening to glance at Dr Dan, saw that his face had changed.

He was no longer the cool scientist. His jaw was

tight, his eyes were staring, as he looked into that awful pit. A terrible fear seemed to be stamped on his face, but still it was not quite like fear. It was a blank expression, a frozen look.

Hal wondered if the man had lost his senses. He was afraid he might step off into space, and put a hand on his arm. He found the body as rigid as a marble statue.

The doctor did not look at him, did not seem to know that he existed. He did not move a muscle.

Hal tried to shake him, but he seemed to have turned into stone. The cheekbones stood out, the neck muscles were tight, the hands were clenched.

So he stood for two long minutes.

Then a little colour crept back into the pale cheeks, the arm that Hal was holding relaxed, and the doctor's eyes moved. He glanced at the hand that gripped his arm and then at Hal and smiled doubtfully, as if wondering why Hal was holding on to him. Hal released his hold. The doctor pointed to a lava fountain at the bottom of the pit and once more he was the calm and interested man of science. He evidently had no memory whatever of those two terrible minutes.

Asama means Without Bottom, and for centuries

the Japanese believed that the volcano had no bottom. But during recent years the bottom has been steadily rising and could now be plainly seen about six hundred feet down.

There, fountains of white-hot lava shot up into the air. Some rose as high as the crater's edge, then fell back. Others kept on climbing thousands of feet into the sky and fell on the mountaintop, with great danger to the volcanologists.

Below the fountains was a boiling white lake of liquid stone. It churned and rolled like the rapids of a great river. Pockets of gas exploded and burst into flame. Huge rocks were hurled up against the sides of the crater and fell back only to be hurled up again. Small stones by the thousand leaped up half a mile into the sky as if shot from a gun. Everywhere steam spurted out of cracks like smoke from the nostrils of a dragon. The din was terrific. The boys put their hands over their ears.

But the doctor did not seem to mind. He focused his pyrometer on the crater floor. Its temperature was 2500 degrees Centigrade. He made notes. Then he pointed to a patch of yellow and orange on the inside slope of the crater about fifty feet down. The noise slackened for a moment and he was able to say,

'I'm going down to take a look at that.'

He unslung the coil of line that he carried on his shoulder. Although small, light rope, it was nylon and very strong. He looped one end of the rope around him under his arms and gave the rest of the coil to the boys.

'Just let me down easily,' he said.

He stepped over the edge and down the steep slope, the hot ashes sliding under his feet. The boys paid out the line. When he slipped they braced themselves and checked his fall.

He reached the colourful deposit of minerals and studied it with his spectroscope. The boys held the line taut. Hal couldn't help thinking, what would happen if a blob of sizzling lava should fall on the line and burn it in two?

The doctor looked up and signalled that he was ready to come back. He scrambled up through the sliding ashes while the boys hauled in on the line.

When he stood beside them again they were breathless from exertion and excitement, but he seemed quite unaffected by his descent into a blazing volcano.

It was about a mile around the crater's edge and finally they came near the spot from which they had started. They looked for the three Japanese men but the smoke from the volcano now drifting around them cut down visibility.

Suddenly, through the smoke two figures came running after them. They recognized Toguri and Machida. Both were greatly excited.

'You come,' Toguri called. 'You come – quick – see.' They turned and ran back into the smoke, Dr Dan and the boys following them. They stopped beside something blue that lay in a heap on the ground.

4

The Discouraged Student

It was a coat. The blue coat of a school uniform. Hal picked it up. He guessed at once what had happened.

'Was Kobo in trouble?' he asked Toguri. 'He seemed very unhappy.'

'Kobo take English examination,' said Toguri. 'He fail – no good.'

Hal wondered how anybody could pass an English examination with such a teacher as Toguri.

They all went to the edge of the crater and looked down. It was impossible to see anything, the smoke was in the way.

'We go,' Toguri said. 'We go – tell his mother.'

'Wait,' said Dr Dan. 'He may still be alive. I'll go down and see.'

The Japanese stared in disbelief.

'Go in crater?' exclaimed Toguri. 'No can do.'

'He may not have fallen all the way down. Perhaps he landed on a ledge.' Dr Dan uncoiled his line and began to knot the end about him.

Hal looked again into the pit. The sun was well up

now and already very hot, but still it did not penetrate that pall of smoke. The thought of going blindly into that crater made Hal sweat. But if Kobo was down there, it was Hal's fault – or so he felt. He blamed himself because he had not gone back to Kobo when he saw that something was wrong.

'Give me that rope,' he said to Dr Dan. 'It's my turn to go down.'

The doctor protested. But when he saw that Hal was determined, he looped the rope about his chest.

Hal wiped the sweat from his face. The heat from the crater with the heat from the sun made him a little sick. The gases from below smothered him.

'Here we go!' he said. 'Hold tight!'

He backed gingerly over the rim. At once he began to slip in the ashes, but the others braced themselves against the pull of the rope and held him up.

He raised his eyes for the last time to the faces of his brother, the doctor, and the two Japanese men, all at the rope. Would he ever see them again – these four?

Four? There seemed to be five. He counted again. The gases made his eyes smart and the smoke made it hard to see. But there were certainly five. Four at the rope, and one standing behind them looking over their shoulders, an expression of great curiosity on his face. The fifth man said in halting English,

'What you do?'

The four turned to face him. They were so startled that they almost dropped Hal into the crater. Hal scrambled up to safe ground.

'Kobo!' he exclaimed. 'You're all right!' Kobo looked blank.

'You had us worried,' Dr Dan said. 'We thought you were down there.'

'Very sorry,' Kobo struggled in English, and then explained in rapid Japanese to Toguri. Toguri passed on his explanation.

'He say too hot here so he go back there – sit – think. He pretty sad.'

'Why does it hit him so hard?' Hal wanted to know. 'In our country lots of boys fail and it doesn't worry them too much. They just try again.'

'Ah, you no understand,' said Toguri, and he went on to tell Kobo's story. Kobo's father had died in the war. His mother and sister were working very hard to put Kobo through school. The least he could do was to succeed in his studies. When he failed he was very much ashamed. He had let his mother and sister down. All the neighbours would have contempt for him. He couldn't bear to go home. He didn't know what to do.

Hal looked into the face of the young student.

Something there appealed to him very strongly. This was a fine boy. He loved his mother and sister and felt deeply disgraced because he had not been able to do his part. He looked bright enough – he would probably pick up English very quickly if he were with people who spoke it well.

Hal took the doctor and Roger aside.

'Listen,' he said: 'I have an idea. How long are we going to be in Japan?'

'About a week,' said Dr Dan.

'That's not very long. But still I think it might be enough. He's eager to learn.'

'What do you have on your mind?'

'If we can take Kobo along with us and talk English with him sixteen hours a day every day, I believe we could teach him more in a week than Toguri could in a year. Then if the school could give him another chance at the examination, he ought to be able to pass it.'

Dr Dan thought for a moment, then smiled. 'You're

a good lad, Hal, and I think your plan might work. It all depends on whether the exam can be repeated. Let's ask the teacher. Toguri-san, could you step over here for a moment?'

Toguri, when told of the plan, was delighted. Yes, he was sure that the school would allow Kobo another examination. 'School know I am very bad English teacher,' he said humbly. 'I know I very bad English teacher. But school no can afford good English teacher. Englishman or American cost too much. We do best we can. One week with you – I think Kobo pass examination.'

'How about Machida?' Hal asked.

'Oh, Machida science student. He no study English.' They went back to Kobo and Toguri told him of Hal's plan. Kobo could not believe it. Why should strangers and foreigners do this for him? He stood looking at Hal and his thanks were in his eyes but he could not think of the right words. Two large tears ran down his cheeks. He smiled through his tears and managed to say:

'I very thank.'

'He go home with me,' said Toguri, 'tell his mother – then come meet you in Tokyo. Yes?'

It was so agreed.

'Now that that's settled,' said Dr Dan, 'let's get out of here. I don't trust this volcano. It's been too quiet for the last half-hour. I think it's getting ready to give us a bath of hot lava!'

They started down the mountain, but by a different route, because Dr Dan wanted to visit the place where lava had buried forty-eight villages.

As they went, the volcano god began to roar again as if angry that these six juicy morsels of food were escaping him. The doctor stopped every once in a while to plunge the spike of his thermometer into a bed of hot ashes. The top layer was only uncomfortably warm, but three inches below the surface the bed was twice boiling hot.

'We could fry eggs here,' said the doctor, 'if we had any to fry.'

Which reminded them that they were hungry again and they stopped to consume the rest of the chocolate bars, rice and fish. While having their lunch they did not sit down, nor even stand, but kept dancing about so that their feet would not be burned.

Then the doctor hurried them on. The growls of Asama were growing louder.

5
The Strong Man

Although down hill, it was hard going. The heat beat down from the sun and up from the ground. It was necessary to climb over large blocks of lava. Most of them were solid and probably weighed many tons, but Roger was astonished when he bumped against one as big as a horse and it moved. It seemed to be riddled with small holes like a honeycomb.

A mischievous idea came into Roger's head. He liked to play tricks upon his older brother who was so much stronger and wiser than he.

They stopped to rest for a moment. Roger said, 'Hal, are you all right?'

Hal stared. 'What do you mean – all right?'

'Aren't you sick or something?'

'Of course not. Why?'

'Well, you just look so pale and weak. I'm afraid this trip has been too much for your delicate constitution. You look tired out.'

'Me tired? You're crazy. If anybody gets tired it

45

will be you, you little shrimp. We'll probably have to carry you home on a stretcher.'

'Well,' said Roger, 'we can easily find out who's tired. How big a rock can you pick up and throw down the hill?'

Hal looked about him. He selected a lava block as big as his head. He got his hands under it, hoisted it with some difficulty, and threw it down the slope.

'There,' he said. 'If you can lift anything half as big as that I'll crown you king of the May.'

'I think I'll try this one,' Roger said, and put his arms around the block as big as a horse.

Hal was much amused. 'Don't make me laugh, kid. You couldn't even budge that, let alone lift it.'

Roger braced his back, tensed his sturdy young muscles and straightened up with the great block in his arms. Then he threw it down the mountainside.

Hal was speechless. He stared at Roger, then at Dr Dan who was laughing.

'Impossible,' muttered Hal. 'Impossible.'

'A very good demonstration, Roger,' Dr Dan said, still laughing. 'Let's go down and take a look at that boulder.'

When they reached it, Dr Dan put his hand on it

and rocked it back and forth as easily as if he had been rocking a cradle. It was as light as if it had been made of paper instead of stone.

'Pumice,' Dr Dan said. 'The rock that floats. Yes, it will actually float on the water. The lightest rock in the world.'

'Does it come from the volcano?'

'Yes. It's really just lava – lava turned into foam. You know how light water is when it is turned into foam. That is because it is full of bubbles each containing air. Well, this is rock foam. It also is made up of bubbles, each containing air or other gases, some of them lighter than air. Some of the bubbles have burst and that's what makes all those holes.'

'But does it really float on the water, like a raft?' Roger wanted to know.

'It does. When the volcano Krakatoa erupted, so much pumice was thrown out on the sea that it made a great floating island three miles across. Some people thought it was a solid island and built their houses on it. One morning they woke to find that a storm during the night had carried their island away over the sea far out of sight of any land. After eighteen days they were rescued by a passing ship.'

'I'd like to take a ride on a pumice raft.'

'You may have a chance when we get to studying the submarine volcanoes. Just now I think we'd better walk rather than talk. I don't like the sounds coming from that volcano.'

They scrambled on down the mountainside. But the boys were too much interested in the stories the volcano man could tell them to allow him to walk in silence.

'What makes a volcano, anyhow?' Roger asked.

Dr Dan smiled. 'Well, that's a pretty big question. Have you ever gone down in a mine?'

'Yes, we went down in a coal mine in Pennsylvania.'

'Was it warm or cold?'

'It was hot. The deeper we went the hotter it got. We nearly melted.'

'Exactly. Now if you had been able to go on down, say twenty miles, you certainly would have melted, and you would find everything around you melted too. The rocks would all be turned into hot soup with a temperature of several thousand degrees. The same thing happens in a steel mill where iron ore is heated until it melts and flows like water. Now then, if you step on an orange what will happen?'

'It will crack and the juice will squirt out.'

'Just so. Think of the millions of tons of earth pressing down upon that rock soup. Naturally, if it can find a crack it will squirt out. And that's just what a crater is. A crater is a crack in the earth's surface. The rock soup sees its chance to escape and up it comes. That rock soup is what we call molten lava. Lava is just rock in a liquid state. It may be any kind of rock, or many kinds together – no matter, it is still called lava.

'Of course, when the lava spurts up through the crack it tears away dirt and rocks and stones and sends them flying up into the air along with the lava. If rain water seeps down through the crack it is turned into steam by the terrific heat. And you know how strong steam is – in a locomotive, for instance. The steam in the volcano may cause terrific explosions that kill thousands of people. The explosions may split the crater so that the molten lava flows out in a great river and covers dozens of towns and villages. And that's just what happened here. You are walking right now on the surface of a river of lava a hundred feet deep. Under it are thousands of Japanese houses. And in them are men, women and children, ten thousand people buried for ever.'

'Why for ever?' asked Hal. 'Vesuvius buried Pompeii, but now they have excavated the city.'

'That's true. But Pompeii was buried under ashes, not lava. It was easy to shovel away the ashes. But these forty-eight Japanese villages lie under a hundred feet of solid rock.'

'Is it likely to happen again?'

'I'm afraid it is. Japanese volcanologists believe that Asama is preparing for another great eruption. After my observations today I am inclined to agree with them. The lava lake in the crater is rising at the rate of fifteen feet a year. No one can say with certainty, but it is quite probable that within the next ten years Asama will put on another big show. But before that it will put on plenty of little shows and a little show would be enough to kill the lot of us, so let's hurry along.'

Asama was now roaring like a wild bull and sending up a tongue of yellow flame thousands of feet into the blue sky. Clots of half-solid lava spattered down on the rocks. Each man kept watch above, and dodged when he saw something coming for him.

And even so, a sticky chunk of red-hot paste struck the sleeve of Machida's coat and stuck there in spite of all his efforts to shake it off. The coat burst into flame. Machida whipped it off and beat it against the rocks to put out the fire. He finally succeeded, but there was nothing left of the coat but a black, charred mass. He threw it away.

The six pressed on more anxiously than ever.

'There's an inn at the foot of the old lava flow,' Dr Dan said. 'If we get to it, we'll be all right.'

Great quantities of ashes were now rising from the volcano. They formed a black cloud in the sky. The sun was blotted out. It grew as dark as if it had been late evening instead of noon. Sudden flashes of light stabbed through the darkness.

'Is that lightning?' asked Hal.

'Yes. Lightning and thunder are very common over volcanoes, because the rising heat disturbs the electrical balance of the atmosphere. I wouldn't be surprised if we have rain too.'

Presently it came: a deluge of rain, but not clean and pure as rain should be. It was a mud rain. The ashes in the sky mixed with water came down as mud.

'That volcano god finds plenty of things to do!' complained Roger. 'But I never thought he'd begin throwing mud pies at us.'

Within ten minutes they were plastered with mud from head to foot. They looked more like clay statues than men. They had trouble keeping the stuff out of eyes and mouths. It covered their ears so they could hardly hear each other. It piled up on their feet and made them heavy. It covered the ground like glue and made walking difficult.

The six mud-men staggered on through the unnatural night. What if they should lose their way? Hal looked anxiously at Dr Dan. He hoped that the doctor wouldn't begin to sing and that the strange attack that had turned him to stone at the edge of the crater would not be repeated. They depended upon the doctor to guide them to safety.

But the doctor seemed calm enough as he clambered over the rocks as nimbly as the heavy caking of mud on his body would let him. Toguri also seemed to know the way.

Gradually a light became visible ahead. It turned out to be a lamp in the entrance to a Japanese inn.

What a relief to step under the projecting roof and

be sheltered from that crazy shower of mud! They tried to clap their hands to call the maid. But no sound came from those mittens of mud.

They shouted, '*Ohaiyo!*' There was a pattering of sandals in the corridor and a maid appeared. She cried out when she saw six mud statues standing in the vestibule. More maids appeared and the proprietor, all with cries of concern and sympathetic laughter.

Muddy shoes were removed, feet were tucked into sandals called *zori*, and the six mud-men were hurried straight to the bath. They were shivering with cold, for the heat of the day had vanished when the darkness and rain began.

Off came the mud-plastered clothes and were taken away at once to be washed and ironed.

Then six dirty men poured buckets of hot water over themselves, applied soap generously, and rinsed themselves clean under more bucketfuls of hot water.

Then they stepped down into the bath. There is nothing in the world quite like a Japanese bath. It is a tub of very hot water three feet deep. This one was large, about fifteen feet square, more like a miniature swimming pool than a tub.

You don't go into a Japanese tub to get clean. You

get clean first, then you enter the tub and squat in it so that only your head is above water. And there you soak for a half-hour or more, enjoying the warmth that seems to relax every muscle and nerve in your body, smoothes away your troubles, and leaves you perfectly content with the world and hungry for dinner.

So they happily soaked and relaxed. Then they stepped out to dry themselves and each slipped on a *yukata* provided by the inn, a sort of light-weight kimono, and they were led to the room that had been assigned to them.

Here they sat down on the soft mat-covered floor before an ankle-high table and were soon manipulating chopsticks over a delicious dinner of hot rice, baked fish, fried prawns, wafers of seaweed, a steamed custard of eggs, mushrooms and chicken, and a dessert made of beans in a syrup of sugar and honey.

Dinner over, the maids carried away the tables and the six were left to themselves.

The Japanese felt perfectly at home, but the others found the room a bit strange. It was nothing like the sort of hotel room they were used to. There was not one stick of furniture in it – no chairs, no bed, no table, no telephone stand, no writing desk, no chest of drawers, no dressing table, no carpet, no curtains.

There was also no dirt. The room was spotlessly clean. Even the floor was as clean as a dinner plate for no one ever came into the room with shoes on. The sandal-like zori were left outside in the corridor. The room was floored with straw mats called *tatami*, three inches thick, soft and springy, and as clean as a whistle.

The three Japanese men lazily stretched themselves out on the floor, and the others followed their example. They were surprised to find how good it felt.

'Not bad at all!' exclaimed Roger. 'A lot better than sitting up in a chair when you're tired.'

They talked over the events of the day. Hal drew Kobo into the conversation and painstakingly corrected his faulty English.

6
Stories of the Volcanoes

The mud rain thudded on the tile roof. Already there must be a heavy blanket of mud on the roof. Roger looked up.

'I've always wondered what it would feel like to be buried alive,' he said. 'Perhaps we'll find out.'

Dr Dan laughed. 'I think the rain will finally conquer the mud and wash it away. But of course there's always the chance that it won't. This was the way Vesuvius buried Herculaneum – under a sea of mud.'

'Have you climbed Vesuvius?' Hal asked.

'Yes. It's easy compared with Asama. It's only four thousand feet high. From the top you get a marvellous view of Naples and the bay and the Isle of Capri. And you can look down into a very angry crater. Vesuvius has blown her top many times, and will probably do it again. But the worst was when she buried Pompeii and Herculaneum.'

'What year was that?'

'Only seventy-nine years after the birth of Christ. What a day that must have been! When people came out of their houses that morning they saw a great black cloud over Vesuvius. Flashes of lightning shot through it and the sound of thunder rolled down the slope of the mountain.

'Then there was a violent earthquake. The ground danced, people lost their footing and fell. Great cracks opened up in the streets, so wide that chariot horses could not jump over them.

'The mountain began to shake with explosions. The black cloud rolled down over the city. It became so dark that no one could see more than a few feet away except when a flash of lightning lit up the scene.

'Lava puddings like those we saw today began to fall and burned many people to death. Small bits of pumice showered down. Sulphurous vapours made people choke. Then the shower of ashes began. Tons and tons and tons of ashes. At first people didn't mind them too much. They just waded through them and laughed. The children had great fun playing in them and throwing them about. The ashes were only ankle-deep.

'But they kept on falling. Soon the people were up to to their knees in ashes. They went inside their houses. But the earthquakes began to shake the houses down upon their heads. So they went out into the street again.

'The ashes were up to their chests. Now they really became frightened. They began to leave the city. Some escaped, others were not able to battle their way through the ashes which were now over their heads. They were buried alive.

'Still the ashes came. They covered the houses, and then the theatres, and then the great public buildings. At last there was nothing but a smooth plain of ashes with the city completely buried far beneath.

'That was what happened to Pompeii. What happened to Herculaneum was a bit different, and more terrible. Over this city rain began to come down in torrents. It turned the ashes into mud.

'Here too the people were afraid to stay indoors because the earthquakes were tumbling the houses down around their ears. They went out into the streets and tried to wade their way out of the city. But they could not wade through the mud. It was up to their knees and it was a very sticky kind of mud, like glue or cement.

'It held them fast. They could not move. They cried out for help but no one could help them. The mud rose to their waists, to their necks. It crawled up over mouth and nose, over the eyes, over the top of the head. On, up over the tops of the highest buildings. Still the mud came until it was one hundred and thirty feet deep.

'Then the shower stopped. The mud began to dry into a hard, stony substance, very much like cement. So the people of Herculaneum stood in the streets in their great cement coffin for eighteen hundred years. People forgot that they had ever existed and new towns were built above their heads.

'Now an attempt is being made to excavate these cities. Much of Pompeii has been uncovered, but the cement coffin defies the diggers. They cannot disturb the new towns so they bore tunnels beneath them. They have reached the theatre and several beautiful temples. It is a hard job, and perhaps most of the city will remain sealed for ever.'

'All the things a volcano can do!' marvelled Roger. 'It buries these forty-eight villages under lava, Pompeii under ashes, Herculaneum under mud.'

'But that's not all,' said Dr Dan. 'It can destroy a city without using lava or ashes or mud. Remember how Mt Pelée killed forty thousand people in five minutes?'

'Tell us about it,' prompted Hal.

'It won't take long to tell because it didn't take long to happen. Mt Pelée – you know where it is, on the beautiful island of Martinique in the West Indies – had been growling for days. The people of the city of St Pierre at the foot of the mountain paid little attention to it. They weren't as wise as the animals.

'The wild creatures left the mountain. Even the snakes crawled away. The birds stopped singing and flew to other islands.

'One morning at seven-thirty the volcano stopped growling. There was complete silence. 'Ah,' said one man to another, 'you see we were sensible not to run away. Pelée has quieted down.'

'The silence lasted for fifteen minutes. Suddenly there was a deafening explosion like the roar of thousands of cannon. The whole side of the mountain was blown to pieces. Out came a huge purple cloud that rolled down with the speed of a hurricane upon the city.

'Lightning zigzagged through it and besides the lightning there were brilliant fireworks in the form of serpents and circles. The cloud was made up of burning gases, terrifically hot.

'The people barely had time to speak before the

burning cloud was upon them.

'I said that forty thousand people died in five minutes. It really took less time than that. The effect of the blast was almost instantaneous.

'The wall of fire swept out into the harbour and sank sixteen ships. The water of the harbour was heated almost to boiling point. Only two ships managed to limp away to safety after most of their crew had been killed. The fire hurricane burned the others and hot whirlpools sucked them down.

'Some of the ships were set on fire by rum – can you imagine that? Thousands of casks of rum stored in the city were exploded by the terrific heat. The blazing rum ran in rivers down the streets and out to sea, setting fire to the ships.

'Sailors on the two ships that got away looked back upon a frightful scene. The city was blazing. Houses lay in heaps, great trees had been torn up by the roots. Not a human being moved. Not a human voice was heard. The sailors believed that every last person had perished.

'They were wrong. One man, just one, still lived. He was discovered four days later by rescue parties. He was a prisoner in the city jail. He was locked in a cell so far underground that the gases and flames did not reach him.

'He saw nothing – his cell had no window. But he knew from the noise and heat that something terrible was going on. Then all became quiet.

'For four days he was without food and water, almost without air. He shouted for help. He tried to break the lock of his cell, but it was no use. He counted himself the unluckiest man in St Pierre.

'Then he discovered that he was the luckiest. He was found and brought out into the light and saw the ruins of the city. It was one of the strangest twists of fate in all history – this man who had committed murder and had been condemned to die, was the only one in the whole city to live.'

So the volcano stories continued through the afternoon and evening as they rested in the snug, dry little inn, mighty thankful to be there.

After supper, the maids brought *futons*, thick, heavy quilts, and spread them on the floor. They made a great bed twenty feet wide. Six small, round pillows were placed on the bed and six men crawled in between the quilts.

This all seemed quite natural to the Japanese. But

the visitors, who were taller, found the quilts a bit short and their feet stuck out. However, they curled them up as best they could and were soon asleep.

For some hours there was no sound but the muffled pat-pat of mud on the roof.

It must have been about two o'clock in the morning when a sharp earthquake shook the house with a clattering, crashing sound and a scream split the air – the scream not of a woman but of a man. Hal felt a sudden commotion in the covers and then someone ran over him, still screaming.

Hal groped for the light and switched it on.

Dr Dan, looking very odd in his yukata which was too short for him so that his bare legs projected beneath it, was frantically beating upon the walls with his fists. Then he smashed the wood-and-paper door that led to the garden and was about to step out when he suddenly stopped screaming, turned slowly, and blinked at the light. Five astonished men sat up in their beds and watched him.

A puzzled look passed over the doctor's face. He seemed surprised to find himself out of bed and standing. He turned out the light and crawled in.

'What goes on?' came the half-asleep voice of

Roger. 'Pipe down,' warned Hal.

The others were soon asleep again but Hal lay staring up into the darkness, wondering and worrying about the doctor's strange behaviour.

Why should the man be so terrified by an earthquake? Earthquakes were common in Japan. An average of four a day were reported, though most of them were too faint to be felt except by the seismograph. Especially a man who made a business of volcanoes should be used to such things.

The doctor was no coward – Hall thought of how readily Dr Dan had faced danger during that exciting day. And yet, how about those two awful minutes at the edge of the crater when the doctor had frozen stiff as he looked down into the pit? When it was over he did not seem to remember what had happened but calmly descended into the crater at the end of a rope.

It was all very puzzling. Could it be that at some time in the past the doctor had had a terrible experience in a volcano, had perhaps suffered mental shock or injury to his head or nervous system – something that would explain these moments when he seemed to lose all control of his actions?

To Hal it seemed a dangerous situation – dangerous for the doctor and for Roger and himself. Were they going to explore fire-breathing volcanoes in the company of a half-crazy scientist? If he could just remain himself, there was no finer companion or abler volcano man. But suppose he lost his grip just at some critical moment? A bad accident might result.

Hal wondered if he should talk to Dr Dan about it. But Dr Dan probably didn't realize anything was wrong. If he had had a frightful experience, he would probably rather not talk about it.

It might be better to say nothing to him. You could hardly step up to a man and say, 'You're crazy.' Perhaps this shock, whatever it was, would wear off. In the meantime, thought Hal, he would just have to keep watch over the doctor day and night to prevent him from hurting himself or others.

Anxiously pondering these problems, Hal lay awake the rest of the night.

7
The Diving Bell

Perched on camels, the volcano explorers jiggled and jounced their way up to the edge of another angry crater.

The camel is not native to Japan; these animals had been brought from the Gobi Desert and for years had been used to carry visitors to the top of Mt Mihara.

'What a view!' cried Hal, scanning the sea below, dotted with steamers and sailing ships. Mihara stands on an island at the mouth of Tokyo Bay. At the north end of the bay lay the great city of Tokyo; to the west, blue mountain ranges; to the southwest, the beautiful cone of Mt Fuji. South and east stretched the mighty Pacific, speckled with islands.

But Roger wasn't looking at the view.

'I wish this camel would stop trying to sharpen his teeth on me,' he complained.

The camel was continually turning its head to bite at Roger's legs.

'Don't let him bite you,' warned Dr Dan. 'Camels

don't brush their teeth and their bite is poisonous.'

Toguri and Machida had gone home, but Kobo, after a visit to his mother, had returned to spend a week with the volcano men. He was as happy now as he had been blue before. He kept chattering with anyone who would talk with him and was absorbing English as a sponge soaks up water.

'How about that big surprise you promised us?' Hal asked Dr Dan. 'When are you going to tell us about it?'

Dr Dan laughed. 'Pretty soon you'll see for yourself. But I can tell you a little now. You boys have been down in the sea in a diving bell. What would you think of going down into a burning crater in a diving bell?'

The boys could only stare at Dr Dan. The question took their breath away.

'When I was in Japan a year ago,' went on Dr Dan, 'I was talking with a Japanese friend of mine who is editor of a great newspaper, *Yomiuri*. He was asking about my volcano plans. I told him that I hoped some day to go down into Mihara crater. I would need something like the diving bells that are used at sea. Just as the diving bell is watertight so that it keeps out the sea, this would need to be airtight to keep out the poisonous gases.

'The editor was much interested in my plan. He said his paper would like to work with me to carry it out. The *Yomiuri* would be glad to pay the cost of the experiment because it would make a big story for the paper. If I would tell them just how to do it they would construct the diving bell and have it ready for me on my return to Japan.

'Now they have done as they promised and the bell is waiting at the edge of the crater.'

'Has this sort of thing ever been done before?' Hal inquired.

'A few times. A man named Kerner went down 805 feet into the crater of Stromboli. Another explorer named Richard went down in a sort of wickerwork gondola into the crater of Raoung in Java – but he had a bad accident. The trouble was with his gondola. I think our diving bell will work very much better.'

Hal could only hope fervently that the doctor was right. At least no one could say that Dr Dan lacked courage.

Now the rim of the crater could be seen, a great column of smoke thundering up out of it.

'There it is!' cried Roger. At the edge of the crater a large object of steel and glass glittered in the sun and beside it was the crane that would lower it into the pit and bring it up again. A number of Japanese men were examining the steel-and-glass diving bell. The boys dug their heels into their camels' sides and hurried to the scene.

There they slid to the ground and were introduced by Dr Dan to Mr Sanada, editor of the *Yomiuri*, and his friends.

Dr Dan and the boys examined the diving bell. It was round, stood about seven feet high and was six feet in diameter. The lower part was of steel, the upper part of glass with steel supports. The steel was in two layers with an air chamber between. The glass also consisted of two panes with space between them, the purpose being to keep out the heat. The top was of steel and in the middle of the top was a large iron ring to which the cable was attached.

Dr Dan opened the tightly-fitting steel door and went inside. A heavy asbestos mat covered the floor, and the walls and ceiling were also insulated.

'I think you will find everything in order,' the editor said. 'You see we have put in a telephone so that you can keep in touch with us. If you get into any trouble just tell us and we will draw you up at once. And here is the dog.'

At the end of a leash a small dog whined uneasily as the ground trembled under its feet and the explosions in the crater sent up clouds of smoke.

'What's the dog for?' Hal asked.

'The dog is a surprise to me,' admitted Dr Dan. 'But I think I know why Mr Sanada brought it. I had told him that when the man went down into Raoung he took a dog with him. A dog would warn him if there was any carbon monoxide gas. You see, this very deadly gas has no smell. It is heavier than air and therefore lies low. If any of this gas seeps into the bell it will lie near the floor and the dog will be affected first. When the man sees this happen he can signal to be hauled up before the gas rises in the bell high enough to kill him. It's a good plan – except that it's hard on the dog.'

The little dog looked up at Dr Dan with pleading brown eyes and whined.

'I think I'll take my chances without the dog,' Dr Dan said. 'Now if you'll give me that bag of instruments, Hal, I'll get going.'

'But you're not going alone,' objected Hal.

'Why not?'

Hal could not tell him why not. But the reason why not was very clear in his mind. Suppose the doctor should have one of his strange moments while in the depths of the volcano. Somebody must go with him.

'You might need some help,' Hal said. 'I'll go along.'

'Me too,' chimed in Roger.

Dr Dan smiled at them both. 'I'll make good volcano men of you yet,' he said. 'But you don't seem to realize that this is a dangerous experiment. The bell will go down all right but whether it will come up is another question. Any one of a number of things might happen. If you are still determined to go, Hal, I'll take you. But there will be room for only two – Roger will have to stay topside.'

Roger looked both relieved and disappointed. He was glad not to go down, yet sorry to miss the adventure.

Hal and the doctor took their places inside the bell. The editor shook hands with them as if he expected never to see them again. The door was closed and locked. First Dr Dan tested the telephone.

'Can you hear me, Sanada-san?'

Mr Sanada, with earphones clamped to his head, replied, 'I hear you perfectly.'

'Very well. We're ready to go.'

The crane's motor whirred. The slack of the cable was taken up and the hook came tight on the ring with a clanking sound. The bell wobbled. The two men inside gripped a handrail on the wall to keep their footing.

The bell left the ground and went straight up about ten feet, then it swung out over the crater. There it rested for a moment as if to give its occupants a last chance to change their minds.

Hal had a heavy feeling in the pit of his stomach. He suddenly hated to leave this beautiful upper world and go down into, who could tell what? He looked out to the white sails on the sea, the sweep of the Japanese mainland, and tranquil Mt Fuji in the distance.

The Japanese were looking up from the crater's edge. A little farther along, other visitors were reciting Buddhist prayers and throwing lighted incense sticks into the crater. They were worshipping the gods, gods very much like devils, that lurked at the bottom of the pit.

Hal looked down through a small glass window in the floor of the bell. The sight made him a little dizzy. Red cliffs dropped away to unknown depths. As the swirls of smoke parted he could see hundreds and hundreds of feet down, and still no bottom. He felt as he had in dreams when he had stepped off a high precipice into space. This was almost the same, except that now he was not dreaming. Fire flashed far below, an explosion shook the mountain and the bell swayed. The thought of going down into that awful pit . . .

But the doctor was calling over the telephone, 'Lower away!'

The bell began to descend. The doctor was already busy with his observations. He was looking at his pocket altimeter.

'We are now 2512 feet above sea level,' he said.

The far view disappeared. They were now below the edge of the crater. Down they went past the blood-coloured walls. Here and there were patches of bright green or deep blue. Everything went down in Dr Dan's notebook.

Now and then he called for a halt so that he could study the deposits more carefully. He made readings with his spectroscope. Then he looked again at the altimeter.

'We're one hundred feet down.' On down. 'Two hundred feet.' Down, down. 'Three hundred feet.'

Hal was looking through the floor window. 'There's a ledge of rock projecting from the wall. I'm afraid we're going to strike it.'

'We may just be able to clear it.' Dr Dan phoned to the men above, 'Slowly, please. Very slowly.'

But the bell could not quite get by the ledge. One edge settled on it and the rest of the bell began to tip over into empty space.

'Stop!' called Dr Dan. 'Stop lowering.'

The order was not obeyed quickly enough. The bell tipped farther, suddenly slipped off the ledge and swung out into space. It swung back and crashed into the wall with a shock that jarred and bruised the men and nearly smashed the thick glass. Out it swung again and in for another crash, but not so severe as the first. Three more bangs, and the bell swung without touching the wall.

Hal, clinging to the handrail, forgot his own terror when he looked at Dr Dan's face. It was very pale and the eyes began to stand out strangely.

Hal put a hand on his arm. 'Dr Dan, look! That geyser of hot water shooting out of the cliff. That's something for your notebook.'

The volcano man seemed to come to himself. He turned to look at the geyser and out came his little book. Then he grinned at Hal.

'Ready to go on down?'

'Ready if you are.'

Four hundred feet down. Five hundred feet. Six hundred. Seven hundred. Still no bottom to be seen. Nothing below but the orange of the flames seen through coils of rose and blue smoke.

Eight hundred feet. Nine hundred feet.

As they neared the hidden lake of fire the bell was shaken more and more by the explosions. It was repeatedly thrown against the wall. Hal was thankful that the volcano was really not in violent eruption. If it had been it could have tossed this little steel-and-glass thing half a mile into the air. Hal spoke his thoughts to Dr Dan.

'Half a mile?' said the doctor. 'That would be easy. Mihara could do better than that if she really got down to business. In one eruption she threw rocks bigger than this bell three miles out to sea.

Now there's a strange deposit.'

He was looking at some white object on a flat ledge.

'Skeletons!' exclaimed Dr Dan. 'There must be three or four of them. It must have happened recently. Even the bones will crumble away quickly in this heat.'

Hal wiped the sweat out of his eyes. In spite of the insulation, the heat inside the bell was becoming intense. The flames below were getting much too close. He had been sorry for the people who had fallen or jumped in – now he was beginning to be sorry for himself.

The bell was not descending smoothly, but in jerks. Dr Dan spoke through the telephone.

'Go easy, boys. No jerks. It's not comfortable – besides it might break the telephone wires.'

'The motor is giving us a little trouble,' came the answer. Hal, in spite of the heat, felt a cold prickle in his backbone. What if the motor should conk out entirely and leave them down in the pit!

Another hard jerk, and a snapping sound above. Dr Dan looked up anxiously. He spoke into the telephone.

'Hello! We've descended far enough. Haul us up now! Hello! Hello!'

There was no answer. The wires had snapped. It was easy to understand what had happened. The cable supporting the bell could stand the jerks, but the telephone wires which ran up alongside the cable had not been able to bear the strain.

Did the men above realize that the wires were broken? If so, they would immediately haul up the bell.

But the bell kept going down. It went more smoothly now and the men were probably congratulating themselves on having fixed the motor.

A thousand feet down and still descending. The heat was suffocating. White-hot lava bubbled out of cracks in the cliff. Eleven hundred feet down. Impossible to signal for a stop.

'Our only chance is that they'll try to use the phone and find it doesn't work.'

Twelve hundred feet. Now they could plainly see the lava lake close below. It was a raging sea of orange and vermilion lava, boiling, rolling over upon itself, leaping up in bloody fountains. Mammoth bubbles threw up fireworks around the bell. The explosions were deafening.

Hal felt as if he must cry out. He must scream as the doctor had in the night. He looked at the doctor, expecting to see terror in his face. But the doctor was too busy to be frightened just now. He was making notes. He would probably keep on making notes until the bell sank into the blazing lake.

The bell jerked to a stop. Perhaps the men at the crane had tried to use the telephone and found no connection. The bell wavered and waited for what seemed a long time. Then it began to rise.

Dr Dan pulled out his altimeter, and made a note in his book. He showed the note to Hal.

'Total descent, 1250 feet.'

He grinned with the happiness of a scientist who has done his job well. Whether they would get back safely to the top did not seem to worry him.

It worried Hal a lot. The bell jumped like a scared cat when explosions went off beneath it. The sudden blasts sent it bouncing against the cliff, then spinning and swinging in space. He noticed that at one point the outer layer of glass was broken. If the inner layer also was smashed, the poisonous gases would pour in.

Sky-rockets soared up through the smoke and a

volley of rocks struck the bottom of the bell. There was a long rumbling and then a terrific crash as if a hundred locomotives were meeting head-on. The crater god lifted the bell as easily as if it had been a baseball and hurled it against the cliff. Broken glass tumbled into the bell. Smoke and gas flooded in through the gaping hole.

Hal stuffed his shirt into the hole. It was not a very good cork. Some gas would come through it and around it. But if the crane motor didn't fail and if there was nothing to interrupt their ascent they might reach the top in time.

The light was changing from firelight to daylight. Now and then they could catch a glimpse of the sky through the smoke. But Hal's rising hope was checked when Dr Dan reminded him of the ledge on which they had stuck during the descent.

'We'll strike it again on the way up,' said Dr Dan. 'If we hit it too hard we might break the cable. Too bad I can't telephone those fellows to slow down.'

He had hardly finished speaking when the roof of the cage struck the ledge with a jarring bump and the bell's ascent was checked. Fortunately the cable still held. But the margin of the rocky shelf firmly pressed down upon the roof of the bell so that further ascent was impossible.

'I was hoping we could slide by,' said the volcano man. 'But it doesn't seem to be on the cards. There's not very much that we can do. If we had a boat hook we could push ourselves off. But this tub doesn't seem to be equipped with boat hooks. Perhaps the chaps upstairs will have an idea.'

He tucked the shirt more tightly into the hole.

'Breathe as lightly as you can so that we don't use up the good air any faster than necessary.'

The men above did realize what had happened for they could see the bell clearly when the smoke parted. They tried lowering it a few feet and then raising it. This was done repeatedly, but every time the steel roof caught under the ledge and refused to slip by.

Roger looked anxious, forgetting his own hurt feelings. He had been pretty sore at not being allowed to go down in the bell. He felt that the Japanese men regarded him as only a youngster and of no real importance to the expedition.

'How did they happen to bring you along?' Mr

Sanada had said. 'You can't be more than fifteen years old.'

Roger, big for his age, actually had a year to go yet before he would be fifteen, but he wasn't going to admit it.

'Well,' he said, 'I guess age doesn't matter so much as experience.'

'Oh, so you've had a lot of experience with volcanoes?'

'Quite a bit.' He wouldn't tell the man that this was only the second volcano he had ever seen in his life.

'I suppose it takes a lot of study to become a volcanologist.'

'Yes, it does.'

Mr Sanada was looking at him with new respect. 'I'm afraid I under-rated you. I thought you were just a kid who had come along for the ride. Now I see you're a trained scientist – quite remarkable in one so young.'

Roger turned away to hide a laugh. It was fun bluffing this fellow. But somehow he wasn't quite happy about it. Truth to tell, he was a little ashamed. Oh well, now that he had made the bluff, he would have to live up to it. He tried to look important, and to make scientific remarks about the crater and its boiling contents.

But when he saw the bell in great danger he dropped his pretence and was just an anxious boy worrying about his brother.

After all attempts to get the bell past the ledge had failed, the man at the crane stopped trying. He turned off his motor. The men gazed blankly at each other. Mr Sanada turned to Roger.

'You're a trained volcano man,' he said. 'What do you think we should do?'

Roger felt very small. It there had been a hole as big as a mousehole he would have crawled through it.

'I . . . don't . . . know,' he admitted.

'What do you do in similar cases?'

'Well,' stumbled Roger, 'we . . . usually send a man down. He could push the bell out a couple of inches – then it would get by the rock.'

'Of course!' exclaimed Mr Sanada. 'Why didn't we think of that? We have plenty of rope here and we can let you right down to the ledge.'

'Me!' cried Roger.

'Yes – not that any one of us wouldn't be willing

to go. But this is obviously a job for a man who knows volcanoes.'

Roger gulped. He looked down to the ledge. The stinging smoke and suffocating gases flooded up into his face. He stood up, feeling green and cold. The men were waiting, and Mr Sanada was looking at him curiously.

'Where's the rope?' said Roger.

It was brought and he had it looped about his chest just as he had seen Dr Dan put it on.

Then he stepped to the edge of the crater. He did not look down into it again – he didn't dare. He turned his back to it and, while the men held the line taut, he let himself down over the edge.

Now he was dangling in space like a spider at the end of a thread. Down he went, rather jerkily, past the red wall. The explosions from below terrified him. He thought at that moment that if there was anything he would never want to do it was to be a volcanologist.

The fumes were stifling. If he only had a gas mask! He was being cooked by the rising heat. Luckily there were strong air currents so that occasionally the heat and gas and smoke were carried away from him and then he could take in deep breaths of almost pure air. He made a practice of holding his breath until these moments came.

His feet struck the ledge. Now he was standing on the rocky shelf. He got down on his hands and knees and crept to the edge. The roof of the bell was caught firmly under the rim.

Roger looked up. He could see the men peering down. He signalled for the bell to be lowered. There was a moment's delay, then the bell eased down an inch or two.

Roger lay flat on the shelf, his head and shoulders over the edge. He could reach the roof of the bell. He signalled for the bell to be raised. Up it came, slowly. Roger, with his hands on the rim of the roof, pushed with all his strength. The bell cleared the ledge with an inch to spare and continued its ascent. As it went by, two grinning faces looked out to the boy on the ledge.

Roger was hauled up and arrived at the top a moment after the bell had landed. Dr Dan and Hal were released from their gassy prison. They were very happy, though dizzy and faint from the effects of the gas.

Hal looked proudly at his younger brother. 'Good

work,' he said, and put his arm about the boy's shoulders.

Mr Sanada burst in with:

'How fortunate we had a good man to send down after you! Remarkable – so young, and yet he's made such a study of volcanology, visited so many craters – he was telling us about it.'

Dr Dan looked at Roger and chuckled. Roger blushed to the roots of his hair. What would the doctor think of him? He waited for Dr Dan to tell Sanada just how much he really knew about craters.

He glanced up. But there was no sarcasm on the doctor's face, only a friendly smile, and all he told Mr Sanada was:

'Roger is a good volcano man.'

8
The Boiling Lakes

The good ship *Lively Lady* sailed west.

Behind loomed a volcano sending up a mile-high column of rose-and-blue smoke. It was Mihara, into which Dr Dan and Hal had descended in the diving bell.

Ahead lay more volcanoes. Hal and Roger were not anxious to get to them too soon.

Their adventures on and in Mihara had tired them and they were glad to lie on the deck in the sun. They felt at home. How good it was to be in the arms of the *Lively Lady* once more.

It seemed a long time since they had set out from San Francisco in this gallant little sixty-foot, Marconi-rigged sailing schooner to capture creatures of the deep sea for their animal-collector father.

They had learned much about the Pacific and what goes on beneath its waves. They had found Captain Ike Flint a fine captain and a good friend. Now the ship had been chartered by the American Museum of Natural History for its study of Pacific volcanoes. But Captain Ike remained as master while Hal, Roger and their Polynesian friend, Omo, had been kept along with the ship. Dr Dan Adams believed that though they knew nothing about volcanoes they were strong in body and brain and would be quick to learn.

Hal, as he stretched out wearily in the soft sunlight, hoped the doctor had not been disappointed.

He would have been encouraged if he could have heard the conversation up forward between Dr Dan and Captain Ike.

'They're tough,' the doctor was saying. 'Hal insisted on going down in the bell with me. When we got stuck, the kid came down at the end of a rope and pushed us off.'

Leather-faced little old Captain Ike chewed the stem of his pipe. 'I'm not surprised,' he said. 'After the things I've seen them do, diving for shark and octopus and such, I wouldn't expect them to be scared by a bit o' smoke and gas.'

Dr Dan smiled. 'Captain, have you ever looked down into a crater?'

'Can't rightly say I have.'

'Well, let me tell you it's more than a bit of

smoke and gas. The thundering racket, the heat, the earthquakes, the fountains of fire, the explosions, the flying rocks, the fumes – well, it's hell let loose. And to go down into a crater – it can be pretty terrifying. I once had an experience . . .' Captain Ike waited for him to continue, but the doctor's face had become as still as marble and the eyes were fixed and staring as if made of glass.

'You were saying . . .' the captain prompted. But there was not the slightest movement in the scientist's face or body. For a full minute he remained so. Then his features melted, his eyes moved, and life seemed to flow through him once more.

'Let's see,' he said, 'where were we? Oh, I was telling you about the boys . . .'

But Captain Ike was thinking to himself. 'This poor fellow remembers something that he might better forget.'

Kobo, the Japanese student in search of English, sat beside Hal and Roger and kept them talking in that language. He was learning fast.

Handsome, brown Omo in his perch in the crow's-nest listened to the deck talk as he scanned the shore of Japan, looking for the passage that would take them to their next Japanese volcano.

'Bungo!' he cried at last. 'Three points to starboard.'

The little ship swung to the right to brave the tide rips and whirlpools of the Bungo Channel.

Then Japan's inland sea, probably the most beautiful sea in the world, with its three thousand fantastic islands and its surrounding mountains crowned with old castles and temples, opened up before them.

The ship rounded to port, and ahead lay one of the strangest sights of the world – a whole mountainside bristling with geysers of steam. Among the geysers were houses, for this was the city of Beppu. Beyond rose a column of smoke from Aso volcano.

'I suppose this is the only city on earth,' Dr Dan told the boys, 'where hot water doesn't cost a penny. Poke a hole in the earth anywhere and up comes hot water or steam or both. Every house gets its hot water from underground. The water never stops coming up – taps can be left running all the time, it doesn't matter. No wood or coal is needed in the kitchen stoves. Meals are cooked by steam from below. Factories run by steam. Powerhouses use steam to make electricity to light the city. Beppu is sitting on a red-hot boiler. Some day the boiler may burst, but until it does the people cheerfully use its power to run their city.'

'Judging from those geysers,' said Hal, 'there's more power than they can use.'

'Yes, most of the steam just shoots up into the air and goes to waste. Most of the hot water runs down into the bay. There's enough power here to run all of Japan, if it could be harnessed.'

The ship anchored in the bay close to the beach. Roger rubbed his eyes.

'These people must be headhunters!'

His brother laughed. 'What makes you think that?'

'Look at all those heads lying on the beach.'

Sure enough, a row of human heads lay on the sand. They were all Japanese. Some were the heads of men, some of women. There were children's heads, too. In some cases the eyes were closed; in others, they were open, as if the heads were still alive. Roger's eyes nearly popped out when he saw some of the heads move and begin to talk to each other.

'Come ashore,' said Dr Dan. 'When we get close to them you'll see what it's all about.'

They stepped out on to the dock and down on to the beach. Now Roger could see that the heads had bodies attached to them, but the bodies were buried in sand. Steam rose from the sand.

'Beppu is famous for its sand bathing,' said Dr Dan. 'How would you like to try it?'

It seemed a curious way to take a bath, but the boys were willing to try anything. In the nearby bathhouse they paid a small fee, removed their clothes, put on trunks, then came out on to the beach.

Roger was the first to be buried. An old woman with a shovel dug a grave for him in the steaming sand, then told him to lie in it. He lay down, but immediately jumped out with a howl of pain for the wet sand was almost boiling hot.

All the Japanese heads laughed at him and chattered to each other. He could imagine what they were saying, 'These foreigners – they can't stand much.'

The old woman cried shame upon him. She took him by the arm and pulled and pushed him down into the steaming grave and before he could leap out again she began to shovel sand over him. When a neat burial mound had been raised, and nothing remained visible but his redhot face, she knocked the breath out of him by giving the mound a final whack with the flat of her shovel.

Roger was quite sure he could not stand the sizzling heat for more than five minutes. But by the time the others were buried his pain had merged into blissful comfort, he felt his muscles and nerves untying their knots and time became of no importance. For an hour they all lay stewing happily and were sorry at the end of that time to see the old woman coming with her shovel to dig them out.

'And now to see the boiling lakes,' said Dr Dan. 'Beppu has a dozen of them. The Japanese call them *jigoku*, which means hell. And when you see them you'll think the name fits.'

The first was Blood Hell and it was something to remember. A small lake of blood-red water boiled and rolled, let out great gusts of steam, and threw up jets of red liquid to a great height. 'Iron sulphide,' explained Dr Dan. 'Sometimes it spouts three hundred feet high. And, believe it or not, this bit of a lake is five hundred feet deep.' He busied himself with his instruments and notes.

Then came Thunder Hell. This was a noisy one. It growled, grumbled, hissed and screamed.

Sometimes in the past it had overflowed to bury people and houses under a scalding flood. To prevent it from doing this again, the Japanese had brought in two gods to watch it. On one side of it stood a statue of the Fire God, and on the other, the Wind God.

White Pond Hell was a vivid blue pool six hundred feet deep, continually bubbling with what Dr Dan said was natrium chloride.

A statue of a great dragon stood guard over Gold Dragon Hell. As if this were not enough to keep the waters under control, statues of Buddhist saints had been placed around the pool. The caretaker of the pool took the boys into his house where they saw his wife cooking by steam straight out of the earth.

The snouts of alligators and crocodiles poked up out of Devil's Hell. The great reptiles were kept in this hot water to speed their growth. When they reached full size they would be shot and their skins used to make shoes and jackets.

In Sea Hell picnickers had let down a basket of eggs to boil them in the bubbling water.

Most curious of all was a boiling waterfall. Bathers stood under it with pained expressions on their faces and let the scalding water beat upon their shoulders and backs. This was believed to be a cure for rheumatism

Not only humans liked the hot water, but animals as well. The boys were constantly tripping over snakes and toads that lived along the edges of the lakes, and monkeys swarmed on nearby Monkey Mountain. These monkeys were smart. They would come down to the bay, dive in, and catch fish in their hands. One had been taught to operate a small train that ran around a circular track. Dr Dan and the boys took a ride behind the monkey motorman.

It was nearly dark. 'How about spending the night ashore?' Dr Dan proposed. 'Captain Ike and Omo will take care of the ship. Here's an inn that looks attractive. Kobo, what does it say on that sign?'

The sign was in Japanese. 'It says the name of this place is The-Inn-by-the-Well-by-the-Cedar-Tree.'

Here they spent the night. The rooms were clean, the food good, and the chief attraction was the great tiled bath full of crystal-clear hot water welling up out of the earth and continually running over.

9
The Avalanche

The next day they went to the crater of Aso – a long distance, so the trip had to be made by train. Then a stiff clamber up through lava boulders. At last they stood looking down into a boiling pot half a mile wide.

Hundreds of feet down were thunderous tumbling pools of sulphurous mud sending up geysers of fire. They were like red clutching fingers that barely reached those who stood peering over the edge. Some of the rising clouds were of snow-white steam, others were pitch-black smoke.

The gases were stifling. Everyone got out his handkerchief and tied it across his nose to keep out the stench of brimstone. An icy wind pulled and pushed as if determined to throw them in. Their backs ached with cold while the cooking heat struck them in the face. The doctor made his usual observations and records and the boys helped him whenever they could.

They were glad to get down from the biting cold of

this mile-high mountain to a tea house on the slope, where they drank hot tea and ate curious little cakes filled with sweet bean paste.

Again the *Lively Lady* put to sea, and again she put in to a Japanese port, this time to visit the monster volcano called Sakura-jima.

'*Sakura* means cherry,' said Dr Dan, 'and *jima* means island. Cherry is all right – it describes the colour of the red-hot lava – but island is all wrong. It used to be an island until 1914 when a terrific eruption threw up so much lava that the sea was filled between the volcano and the mainland and the island was turned into a peninsula. The city on the mainland was shaken to bits and one village near the volcano was buried under 150 feet of lava. Ninety-five thousand people lost their homes.'

'Is that the only time she erupted?' Hal asked.

'By no means. Old Cherry has blown up twenty-seven times in the past five centuries.'

'Well, I hope she's all done now.'

'I'm afraid not. They say she's getting ready to stage a new act. Let's go up and see for ourselves.'

The way led at first through orange groves and vegetable gardens. Everything was growing lushly in

the soil kept warm by the fires underneath. Farther up the trees and fields disappeared and there was nothing but savage black rocks. Every once in a while the shaking of the mountain would dislodge a rock and it would come tumbling down, a great danger to climbers.

At last they reached the dropping-off place and looked down into their fourth crater. Old Cherry deserved her name – the waves and fountains of liquid lava were cherryred. They looked very angry and it was easy to believe that they were planning mischief.

The doctor went to work with his instruments, and by now Hal and Roger were able to be of real help to him.

'Let's go around the crater,' suggested Dr Dan. 'There won't be time for us all to make the complete circuit. Suppose we split up – two will go one way and two the other and we'll meet at the far side. Roger will go with me.'

The doctor and Roger struck off while Hal and Kobo went in the opposite direction. There was no path along the edge of the crater and the way was very rough. The lava here had been exploded by gases into glassy fragments as sharp as needles and pins, and when Hal stumbled and fell he came up with his hands full of slivers.

'Not the nicest place in the world to go for a walk!' he said as he picked the sharp points from his hands.

'Not the nicest place to go for a walk,' repeated Kobo, practising his English.

At every step they crushed through a bed of black lava glass a foot deep. Their socks were soon cut to ribbons and their legs bled. The blades of glassy rock were as sharp as razors.

'Obsidian,' Hal said. 'In ancient times before iron was discovered people used to make knives out of this stuff.'

Hal stopped to jot down in his notebook items that he knew the doctor would want to have. He stood still only a moment, but the scorching heat from below came up through the soles of his boots and made him move on in a hurry.

They clambered over ridges twenty feet high that looked like great waves of the ocean suddenly turned to stone. They were panting and puffing now, and sweating at every pore.

'I think we stop little time now, rest,' suggested Kobo, and sat down heavily on a rock. He leaped up at once for the rock was as hot as a stove. They stumbled on along the crater's edge.

Hal suddenly stopped. He was looking down the steep slope into the crater. About thirty feet down gleamed some peculiar blue stones.

'That's something the doctor will want,' said Hal, 'a sample of that rock.'

'But you cannot,' objected Kobo. 'It is too – up and down.'

'You mean too steep? Oh, I don't think so – if I take it slowly.'

'But we have no rope.'

'I think I can manage without one.'

He turned his back on the crater and lay down on his stomach, his feet over the edge. Then he eased himself gradually down the slope, using his hands and feet as brakes. Fortunately the volcanic glass had given way to a sort of gravel that was not so hard on the hands.

He was to learn in a moment, however, that even gravel can be dangerous. Stones that he dislodged with his fingers or feet tumbled down the slope, and kept on tumbling until they splashed into the fiery red lake far below.

Hal had nearly reached his goal when he was suddenly terrified by a new sensation. The whole gravel bed on which he lay had started to slip. If this was a real landslide it would carry him straight to his death in the lake of fire.

He tried to keep his nerve. He knew that if he scrambled upwards he would only make the slide move faster.

He lay perfectly still while his body slipped inch by inch and the stones tumbled past him.

Then the slipping stopped. He did not move. What to do now? If he tried to climb he would start the landslide.

He could do nothing but stay where he was. Even that was dangerous, for his weight might start the gravel moving. He was in a pretty fix. Looking up, he saw that Kobo was starting down towards him.

'Stay where you are,' he cried. 'You'll only make it worse. Go and get Dr Dan.'

He knew as he said it that it was a foolish suggestion. It would take an hour to fetch Dr Dan and this was a matter of minutes. At any second the slide might begin.

'No time get doctor,' called Kobo, and kept on

coming. 'Go back,' demanded Hal. 'You can't do a thing. No use two of us getting bopped off.'

He found himself thinking a crazy thought: if Kobo was 'bopped off' then all the time he had spent teaching the boy English would be wasted.

Kobo was creeping lower. The idiot – he would start everything going and they would both slide down.

But Kobo stopped on a solid flat rock about ten feet above his friend. He called down to Hal.

'Take off your . . .' His English failed him. He slapped his legs. 'Take off – the word, I do not know.'

'What are you talking about?'

'These,' he slapped his legs again. 'Take off.'

'You mean my trousers?'

'Ah, yes – trousers! Take off. Do same like me.' He undid his own trousers and began to slip them off.

He'd gone plumb crazy, thought Hal. Gone clean out of his head.

Suddenly he understood Kobo's plan. Yes, it might work. Very carefully he moved his hands down to his belt. He loosened the belt and the waistband. The stones started moving and he lay still. When they stopped he began inching off his trousers. He took his time about it. Better go slow with this than fast with the avalanche.

At last they were off. He tossed them up to Kobo. He did this as lightly as he could, yet it started a slipping of gravel. Hal slid three inches nearer the hungry fire – then the movement stopped.

Kobo fastened the two pairs of trousers together with his belt. Then he lay flat on the rock and threw Hal one end of the crude lifeline. Hal caught it.

But would Kobo be able to draw him up? Hal was much larger and heavier than him.

Hal did not expect much. Probably Kobo could not lift him. Or the trousers would split, or pull apart. Then he would start sliding and wouldn't stop until he plopped into a bath twenty times as hot as boiling water. And with his trousers off! Well, he wouldn't suffer long.

The heat, the noise, the danger – they made odd notions race through his brain. He didn't want to die with his trousers off. He had heard an old soldier say, 'I want to die with my boots on.' That was the way he would like to die, too, if he had to die – in full uniform, fighting a glorious fight. But to pass out by slipping and sliding half-dressed into a pot

hole – that was no way to die. That was something to make anybody laugh. He could laugh at it himself, and he did. Kobo was astonished to see him laughing.

Another fancy struck him: if he turned up at the pearly gates without his trousers would St Peter let him in?

All this fled through his half-dizzy mind in a moment. Then he heard Kobo calling:

'You big boy. I no can bring up unless you help. I count to three. Then you come like everything and I pull like so. Are you ready?'

'Ready!' replied Hal. His day dreams were gone now and he tensed himself for the big effort.

'*Ichi!*' began Kobo. Hal knew that ichi meant one. In his excitement Kobo had forgotten his English and was counting in his own language.

'*Ni!*' Hal gathered up all his strength. '*SAN!*' yelled Kobo, and pulled.

Hal leaped upward at the same instant. The stones flew out from under his feet. There was a muttering growl and the whole gravel bed upon which he had been lying began to slide. A ripping sound told him that the trousers were coming apart at the seams.

But by now he had his hands over the edge of the solid rock occupied by Kobo.

There he dangled as everything went out from under him. Every stone that slid started another stone sliding. The landslide spread left and right until it seemed that the whole slope was roaring downwards. It thundered like the hooves of a thousand wild horses and clouds of dust rose from it.

The avalanche crashed down into the lava lake making a sound like heavy surf on an ocean beach.

Helped by Kobo, Hal scrambled up on to the rock. Then they turned and climbed on firmer ground to the edge of the crater. Here they looked back on a terrifying sight as the avalanche carried billions upon billions of tons of rock down into a blazing lake so hot that it would almost immediately turn the hard rock into flowing liquid.

Half dazed by their experience they trudged on along the edge of the crater until they met Dr Dan and Roger. As soon as they saw them these two gentlemen began to laugh.

Hal thought, they wouldn't laugh if they knew what we have been through. Then his mind cleared a bit and he realized that something was missing. They had forgotten to put on their trousers. Kobo was still carrying them in his hand. He began to untie them from each other.

The doctor was no longer amused. He could see by the bedraggled and weary appearance of the two boys that something pretty bad had happened. They were bruised and battered and covered with dust.

'We heard an avalanche,' Dr Dan said. 'Were you mixed up in it?'

'We certainly were,' said Hal. 'And I'd be at the bottom right now if it hadn't been for Kobo. Kobo and two pairs of trousers.'

He and Kobo pulled on their badly ripped trousers. Dr Dan was looking at them thoughtfully. Then he turned and started down the mountain with Roger. For a while they walked in silence, each too full of his own thoughts to speak. Then Dr Dan said:

'Well, Roger, I think Kobo has paid for his lessons.'

'I'll say he has!' agreed Roger.

10
The Sinking Ship

Again the *Lively Lady* sailed, this time due south. Japan was left behind.

Left behind also was Kobo who had returned to his school for another examination. Hal anxiously wondered what the result would be. He was to get word later that Kobo had passed with flying colours.

Dr Dan came running up the companionway to the deck. 'Captain! Crowd on every inch of sail. Use the auxiliary too.'

'What's the rush?'

'I've just had a radio call from the Hydrographic Office. They report an eruption about two hundred miles south.'

Captain Ike called to Omo to loose the staysails and start the engine.

'What course?' he asked Dr Dan.

'Set your course for Myojin Island.'

Captain Ike scanned his chart.

'There's no such place. It says here Myojin sank out of sight forty years ago.'

'She's just popped up again.'

Hal and Roger, who had been loafing on the deck, suddenly came to life.

'Are we going to see a big eruption?' inquired Roger.

'According to the seismographs it's so big that if it exploded in the middle of New York, there would be no New York.'

'Who reported it to Tokyo?' Hal asked.

'The captain of a fishing schooner. His ship was nearly buried under ashes. He escaped just in time.'

'Did they tell you anything more?'

'They're sending their own exploration ship to have a look at it. Her name is the *Kaiyo Maru*. She's already on the way with nine scientists and a crew of twenty-two. If we're lucky we may catch up with her.'

'Did you say that the volcano is making an island?'

'Yes. There used to be an island there years ago, then it disappeared. Now a new island is being thrown up.'

'Isn't that unusual – for a submarine volcano to make an island?'

'Not at all. Most of the islands in the Pacific were thrown up by submarine volcanoes. Even the coral islands rest on the rims of old volcanoes.'

'And new ones are coming up all the time?'

'Exactly. There are more than twenty islands in the Pacific now that did not exist fifty years ago. The Pacific, you know, is the most volcanic part of the globe. There are about three hundred active volcanoes in the world, and seven-eighths of them are in or around the Pacific. Probably there are a great many volcanoes beneath the sea that we don't know about and every now and then one of them tosses up an island. Sometimes the island doesn't last. It may disappear again.'

'What makes it disappear?'

'It may be made up mostly of volcanic ash, and in that case the waves will gradually wash it away. If it is made of solid lava it is more likely to stay. But even a solid island isn't safe if there's a volcano under it. The terrific forces in the volcano may push the island higher, or they may shrink and let the island drop beneath the waves.'

Dr Dan picked up the binoculars and scanned the horizon ahead.

'I see it!' he exclaimed. 'The column of smoke.'

Roger grinned. 'I think you're kidding us, Dr Dan. You said it was two hundred miles away. Nobody can see two hundred miles.'

'That's where you're wrong. You can see a million miles.'

'A million miles!'

'Of course. How about the sun and the stars? They are millions of miles away but you can see them very plainly.'

That gave Roger something to think about.

'Now I suppose you'll be asking me another question,' said Dr Dan. 'If we can see the smoke two hundred miles away, why can't we see the *Kaiyo Maru* which is fifty miles or so ahead of us?'

'Oh, I know the answer to that one,' said Roger. 'The ship is too low - the curve of the earth hides it. The smoke cloud is very high.'

'Right. At least two miles high.'

'When do we get there?'

'Perhaps early tomorrow morning. What speed are we making, Captain?'

'Seventeen knots.'

'A wonderful little ship!' said Dr Dan.

The *Lively Lady* trembled as if with pleasure at this compliment. She vibrated like a harp with the pull of the wind on the sails. She flew over the waves like a flying fish.

She was no ordinary fishing schooner. She did not carry the usual gaff mainsail. She was equipped with the fastest sail in the world, the triangular Marconi. There was no foresail. Instead, between the two masts, billowed two great staysails. A big jibsail bulged over her bow. She was built for speed and had won several cup races.

They overhauled the *Kaiyo Maru* just before dark. The steam-driven vessel was plodding along at about ten knots. The *Lively Lady* skimmed past her like a bird. The boys were very proud of their swift ship.

True, if the wind failed she would stand still, while the steamer would keep plodding along. But with the right wind the sailing ship was hard to beat.

Passing close to the other ship, the boys lined the rail and waved. At the rail of the steamer stood the nine scientists and some of the crew. Compared with the *Lively Lady*, the steamer seemed so slow that Roger couldn't help calling, 'Get a horse!'

If he had known that every man on that ship would be drowned before another day passed he would not have felt like joking.

The Japanese at the steamer's rail grinned back and shouted admiring comments on the appearance of the *Lively Lady* and its speed. Then their ship was left behind and the growing darkness slowly blotted it out.

'We'll be the first to get there!' exulted Roger. There was little sleeping done that night. Every hour or so the boys came on deck to look ahead to the pillar of cloud and fire.

As they drew nearer it seemed to grow larger and taller. It threw out arms and the top was shaped like a head, so that you could imagine it was a great giant breathing fire and fumes and getting ready to pounce upon the little sailing ship. The *Lively Lady* seemed very much alone now in this great black sea with the evil giant as high as the sky looming over it.

Roger was no longer sure that he wanted to get there first. He wished now that the *Lively Lady* had slowed down so that they might have had the other ship for company.

Blinding flashes of lightning ripped through the cloud and shot down into the sea. Suppose one of them should strike the *Lively Lady*? Thunder came in sudden smacks and whacks as if a dozen giants were clapping their hands. Along with this come-and-go thunder, caused by electrical discharges in the cloud, there was the steady thunder of the submarine volcano itself as it sent millions of tons of boiling lava and white-hot rocks spurting up into the sky.

'How deep is that volcano under the sea?' Roger asked Dr Dan.

'We don't know yet. From the way it's behaving, I'd guess it to be perhaps three hundred feet down.'

'So all that hot stuff has to shoot up through water three hundred feet deep?'

'That's right.'

'Why doesn't the water put out the fire?' Roger grinned to himself. Now he thought he had asked one the doctor couldn't answer.

'That's a good question,' Dr Dan said. 'Ordinarily water does put out fire. And it doesn't take three hundred feet of water either. Just a spray of water may put out the fire in a burning house. But that's because the fire isn't very hot. It's hot enough to burn wood, yes, but not hot enough to turn metal into liquid. The heat in the earth is at least ten times as great. It turns solid rock into liquid. When that blazing liquid shoots up through the water it changes every drop of water it touches into steam. So you see, instead of the water cooling the fire, the fire boils the water. Most of that great cloud is steam.'

A zigzag dagger of lightning split the sky and struck the water within a few hundred yards of the *Lively Lady*.

'I think we're close enough,' suggested Captain Ike.

'How about heaving to until daylight?'

Dr Dan agreed.

The *Lively Lady* came up into the wind. The staysails and jib were lowered and the mainsail flapped idly.

It was a terrible two hours until daylight, the roaring and gigantic bubbling of the submarine volcano and the crash of thunder in the towering cloud made sleep impossible. The flashes of lightning in the cloud were like sudden fireworks. For an instant they lit up the sea for miles. Then the sea went black again. But the two-mile-high column always glowed with the light given off by the streams of white-hot lava shooting up into it.

The *Lively Lady* was no longer moving forward, but she was not lying still. She hopped and leaped like a frightened deer. Every explosion of the volcano sent tidal waves rushing over the sea. They picked up the ship and tossed it into the air, then let it fall deep into a trough. They collided with the ocean's own waves and sent up great jets of spray.

Crash! The worst explosion yet shook the sea.

'I'm afraid that will start a big roller,' said Dr Dan 'Better lash yourselves to the rail or the rigging.'

They made themselves fast and waited. Several minutes passed.

'Guess it was a false alarm,' said Hal.

'Don't be too sure. It takes a little time for it to get here.'

'Look!' cried Roger. 'What's that coming?'

It was like a moving wall. It towered black against the column of fire. It seemed as high as the masts. It was bending over the ship.

The men curled themselves into balls to withstand the shock. The wall of water broke over them. Hal's lashings were torn apart and he was swept across the deck to the rail. There he clung desperately. The ship layover on her beam ends. Would she completely turn turtle?

She would not. The brave little ship righted herself and the water drained away from her deck.

'Boy, was that hot!' cried Roger, when he could get his breath. 'I feel like a boiled eel.'

He got no answer through the dark from his brother. He called anxiously.

'Hal, are you there?'

Hal, who had been bruised when flung against the gunwales, replied rather weakly, 'Yes, I'm here. But I came near leaving you for good.'

'Tie up again,' warned Dr Dan. 'There's more to come.' The following waves were smaller but just as hot. They scalded the skin and made the men choke and gasp for breath.

Then something solid struck Roger in the face. He grabbed it. It lay limp in his hands.

'Now they're throwing fishes at us,' he called.

'Yes,' answered Dr Dan. 'I've had several of

them. Hang on to them. We'll cook them for breakfast.'

'But why are they coming aboard?'

'They're paralysed by the heat. It makes them float to the surface. This would be a wonderful place for a fleet of fishing schooners just now. They could get thousands of tons of fish with no trouble at all. Do you hear the birds?'

The air was full of the scream of gulls and terns as they wheeled about over the dark waters.

'They've come to pick up the fish. But it's a dangerous place for birds, too. I think they are going to be sorry that they were so greedy.'

The sky was turning from black to blue. As the dawn came a strange scene was revealed to the men on the *Lively Lady*.

The giant of steam, gas, smoke and flying lava towered to the sky. It was made up of rolling billows and puffy pillows like a thunder cloud, but whoever saw a thunder cloud standing on the water and rising two miles high? Its hair was braided with snaky shafts of lightning and thunder rolled down its sides.

The sea was not made of waves as the sea should

be. It was humping and jumping, sending up hills of water with sharp peaks. Steam drifted from the peaks. The whole sea was bubbling with the escape of gases from beneath. Geysers of gas and steam shot up here and there.

Not far away a big whirlpool swept round and round. A wall of water circled it and at its centre was a deep hole. If a ship as small as the *Lively Lady* got caught in that whirl it would go straight down to Davy Jones' Locker.

'I never saw so many fish in my life,' exclaimed Roger. On every side were the upturned white bellies of fish that had given up their fight for life in the scalding water. Most of them were small, a foot or two in length.

'The small ones feel it first,' said Dr Dan. 'The big fellows can stand it a while longer. There's one now.'

A great shark that must have been twenty feet long raced through the water gulping down dozens of fish. Presently the boys sighted another shark, and then another. Their huge jaws opened and their teeth as big as spearheads crunched a dozen fish at a time. Blood stained the water, attracting more sharks.

'I hope we don't get dumped into that sea,' said Hal fervently. 'I'm willing to let the sharks have it all to themselves.'

But the sharks were not left to enjoy their breakfast alone. Thousands of birds sought to seize the fish before the sharks could get them. Petrels, terns, gannets, gulls, kittiwakes, wheeled and screamed and boldly plucked their breakfast, even from the open jaws of sharks. They were all wildly excited.

Very calm by contrast was a great albatross with a wing span of seven feet that glided smoothly down, plucked up a fish in its great curved beak, and soared up again without bothering to flap its wings. The smaller birds scattered quickly out of its way.

'And what's that big black one?' Roger asked.

'A man-of-war bird,' said Dr Dan. 'Isn't he a whopper? He must be ten feet across. See what he's doing!'

The man-of-war bird did not bother to go to the sea for his breakfast. He snatched it from the beaks of the smaller birds. He went around like a tax collector demanding payment from every bird that came near him with a fish in its mouth. The gulls scolded and the petrels whined, but it did no good.

One saucy tern hung on to its fish tightly when the man-of-war tried to tear it from its beak. The big bird had an answer for that one and calmly gulped down both the fish and the tern.

The man-of-war had another strange trick. He seized a gannet that had already swallowed its fish and squeezed the smaller bird so hard that the fish popped out. Then he made a swift lunge and caught the fish before it reached the water.

Then with a flirt of his tail he pursued a petrel. But it was a thin petrel and the big bird evidently decided that it contained no fish; he turned away and chased a plump kittiwake, caught and squeezed it, and got another fish.

'How mean can you get!' said Roger.

The sun came up like a red ball of fire in the smoky sky. Dr Dan was using his binoculars.

'The *Kaiyo Maru*!' he said.

Within an hour the Japanese ship had arrived. She did not draw close to the *Lively Lady*, for the tossing sea might have crashed the two ships together. But there were friendly waves and shouts between the two vessels, then the *Kaiyo Maru* steamed closer to the eruption.

'What are they going to do?' asked Roger.

'Make a survey. You see, that ship belongs to the Hydrographic Office in Tokyo. You understand what that means?'

'Not quite,' admitted Roger.

'"Hydro" means water and "graphic" means to write. It's the business of a hydrographic office to write down information concerning the waters – oceans, lakes, rivers. The charts Captain Ike is using were made by the U.S. Hydrographic Office. The Japanese make similar charts and when a new island appears they have to send out scientists to measure it. They find out how long it is, how wide it is, how high it is, how deep the sea is around it and so forth. All this information will appear on the next chart that is printed. Ships' captains wouldn't dare sail without these charts – so you see how important the work of the hydrographers is.'

'I don't see any new island.'

'It's hard to see because of the smoke. Take these binoculars and look just at the foot of the cloud. Now can you make it out?'

'Oh, that big black thing! I thought that was a cloud. Why, it must be a mile or two long. And a couple hundred feet high.'

'And growing every minute,' put in Dr Dan. 'And a week ago there wasn't anything there but water. Captain, suppose we sail around the island.'

'Okay,' said Captain Ike, 'provided we keep at a respectable distance. I'm not hankerin' to lose my ship.'

It was a strange passage as the *Lively Lady* sailed through a sea of floating fish and the clouds of screaming birds.

Most spectacular were the leaps of the makos. The mako is the greatest jumper of all sharks. Catching sight of fish on the surface, they would come up from the deeps at terrific speed, snatch their food and, unable to stop, would shoot ten or fifteen feet into the air. Then they would come down with a heavy splash and disappear.

One shot up so close to the ship that when he fell he nearly struck Roger who was standing at the rail. Roger jumped back just in time. The big shark smashed the rail to smithereens, then fell into the sea.

Hundreds of birds, too full to swallow anything more, perched on the masts and rigging and on the upper edges of the sails and whined mournfully at the sight of so much food that they were unable to eat.

A changing wind made the gigantic column lean over the ship. Ashes and cinders began to shower down upon the deck. Many of them were burning hot and started small fires which the men quickly put out.

Captain Ike came back to speak to Dr Dan. The captain's face was drawn and anxious.

'Doc, how soon can we get out of here? I don't like this a bit.'

Dr Dan looked up from his instruments and notes. 'I'd like to watch this a while longer. It's very interesting.'

'Interesting my hat!' grumbled Captain Ike as he went forward. He could not understand the scientific man's passion for acquiring knowledge about the strange forces of nature.

The wind carried the smoke over the ship and the sun was obscured. It grew as dark as evening although it was not yet noon. The gases that were mixed in with the smoke and steam made the men choke and cough. The birds flying above were overcome by the gas and began to fall in showers upon the deck.

Through the half-dark could be seen the *Kaiyo Maru* sailing close to the volcanic island. Then a cloud of steam and smoke hid it from view.

Suddenly the sea began to shake violently and the ship trembled and bounced.

'Earthquake,' said Dr Dan.

There was a rumbling sound that steadily grew louder. It was like the roll of drums in a great orchestra. It became deafening and Roger clapped his hands over his ears.

Up it seemed to come from the centre of the earth, up, up, rolling louder and louder, until it ended in a gigantic crash that seemed as if it must be enough to blow the world apart.

A monstrous fountain of fire burst up out of the sea and climbed up into the cloud. A blast of hot air struck the ship and heeled her so far over that her starboard rail was under water. The men clung like monkeys to the rigging. The ship righted herself with difficulty.

'Point her up!' Dr Dan shouted to the captain. 'Tidal wave coming.'

Such an eruption was bound to start a tremendous wave. It would have to be faced head-on. The *Kaiyo Maru*, closer to the volcano, would feel it first.

Dr Dan strained his eyes to catch sight of the other ship. Billows of steam rolled aside and he saw it, wallowing in a bad sea. The ship was broadside to the volcano. She was evidently trying to come around to point in, but would she have time to make it before the big wave arrived?

'I'm afraid that ship is in for trouble,' Dr Dan said. 'There comes the wave.'

Even without binoculars Hal and Roger could see it – a towering bank of solid water rushing from the eruption toward the *Kaiyo Maru*. It buried the ship completely out of sight, then came tearing on to do the same for the *Lively Lady*.

But by the time it arrived it had lost part of its power and the little ship had turned and was ready to take it head-on. The men had lashed themselves fast. They took a long breath as the water thundered down upon them, for it was the last breathing they would be able to do for a while.

They were under twenty feet of water. This was deepsea diving without any of its pleasures. They felt the water tearing past them, trying to wrench them from their fastenings.

Dead birds that had been lying on the deck were picked up by the flood and flung in their faces.

It was the longest sixty seconds they had ever known before the little ship came up like a submarine and rode on the surface once more.

Dr Dan's first thought was for the *Kaiyo Maru*.

'There she is!' he cried. 'Bottom up. Captain . . .'

But Captain Ike did not need to be told to go to the rescue. He had already had the *Lively Lady* moving towards the wreck. Only the upside-down keel of the *Kaiyo Maru* could be seen. As they came nearer they could see bits of wreckage floating in the water with a few men clinging to them.

But only a few. Where were all the rest? There had been a crew of twenty-two, and nine in the scientific staff. Most of them must be imprisoned inside the ship.

Another big wave, smaller than the first, rolled in. When it had gone by there were still fewer men clinging to wreckage. Would the *Lively Lady* be in time to save anyone?

The great blast of fire had started hurricane winds.

They came straight for the *Lively Lady* as if determined to prevent her work of rescue.

The Japanese ship was settling lower and lower. Finally it disappeared beneath the waves carrying its prisoners with it.

Now only one man could be seen, clinging to a spar. The tumbling waves dashed him here and there, but he hung on. The *Lively Lady* hauled in close to him. A line was flung, but failed to reach.

Before it could be thrown again, the wind picked up the *Lively Lady* and tossed her back on her haunches, then spun her round and carried her swiftly out to sea. So lightly did it spin her along that she might have been a chip instead of a ship. In vain did Captain Ike try to bring the helm around. Nothing that man could do was equal to the strength of the hurricane.

Not till they were far out to sea did the wind suddenly drop; then a dead calm succeeded it.

'Shall we go back after that man?' Hal asked.

'No use,' said Dr Dan. 'I saw him go under just as the wind struck.'

The tragedy weighed heavily upon their hearts. How sadly the news would be received in Tokyo. But a message must be sent, and Dr Dan sent it.

From Tokyo it was relayed to the hydrographic offices of other nations. So it happened that some weeks later the following notice appeared in the U.S. Hydrographic Bulletin:

KAIYO MARU

The Hydrographer notes with deep regret the sinking of the Japanese Hydrographic Office survey vessel *Kaiyo Maru*, with the loss of all on board.

The *Kaiyo Maru* had been dispatched to survey the newly-discovered Myojin Reef which had appeared as a result of a volcanic explosion. In addition to her regular complement of twenty-two, under the command of Capt. Harukichi, she carried nine scientists, including Dr Risaburo Tayama, Chief of the Surveying Section; Mr Terutoshi Nakamiya, Chief of the Oceanographic Section; Mr Minoru Tsuchiya, Assistant Chief of the Surveying Section; and Dr Kiyosuke Kawada, Assistant Professor of Tokyo Education University. Aside from a few pieces of wreckage, no trace of the vessel has been found. It is presumed that volcanic action contributed to the loss of the ship.

The Hydrographer expresses the condolences of the United States Navy Hydrographic Office to the Japanese Hydrographic Office and the families of the men who gave their lives in the advancement of science and marine safety. In this disaster, the maritime world has suffered a severe loss.

The notice was boxed within a heavy black line. That black border meant sympathy, the sympathy one man has for another, no matter whether they be of the same nationality or the same race. For men of science the world around know only one race – the race to learn the facts of the universe, and they will let no danger stop them in their quest for truth.

11
Diving to the Lost Island

'Who would have thought there could be so many volcanoes under the ocean?'

Hal was perched in the crow's-nest with Dr Dan. From this point high up the foremast of the *Lively Lady* they could see spurts of steam rising from the sea. They looked like the spoutings of whales but really came from underwater craters. There was a constant rumbling sound and the smell of sulphur. Rocky islands dotted the ocean.

'They are called the Volcano Islands,' Dr Dan said. 'You can't see some of them because they are under the surface. We are sailing over an island right now.'

'Sailing over an island!'

'Yes. It poked its head above the waves in November 1904. It was a rocky island with a circumference of two miles and had a fine pumice-stone beach. These islands were Japanese at that time and Japan was very proud of her new island. But it lasted for only two years, then sank out of sight.'

'See that smoke on the horizon ahead? Perhaps it's a steamer.'

'No, I think it's another volcano. It's name is Uracas. While some islands are sinking, that one is rising. It's already more than a thousand feet high and still growing.'

They did not reach Uracas until late at night. The boys tumbled out of their bunks and came on deck to look at it.

Ashes were showering down on the deck. The ship was trembling from the shock of the explosions.

Uracas was a thousand feet of fire, topped by a column of smoke that went up several thousand feet more.

The mountain wore a white-hot coat of flowing lava that sizzled and roared as it struck the sea. The illuminated mountain lit up the sea for miles.

The volcano was shaped just as one would imagine a volcano should be, tapering steeply up to the crater. Its perfect toboggan-slopes were kept smooth and straight by the frequent flow of lava and ashes.

Roger was puzzled. 'What's that at the top – snow?'

It did look as if the volcano were wearing a cap of snow. 'White sulphur,' said Dr Dan.

The streams of blazing lava ran down over the white cap and then over the coal-black cinder slopes to the sea. The steam that rose when the lava struck the water glowed with the light from the blazing stream so that the whole volcano seemed to be floating on a bed of fire.

The glowing column of smoke turned and twisted like the tongue of a great dragon licking the night sky. Every few minutes another explosion came, throwing up fiery gobs of lava and burning ashes into the cloud.

'Sea captains call it the lighthouse of the Pacific,' Dr Dan said. 'They use it to check their bearings. It can be seen more than a hundred miles away – its column of smoke by day and its pillar of fire by night. Have you ever heard of Stromboli? It's called the lighthouse of the Mediterranean. It stands in the sea near Naples and throws up blazing lava every ten minutes. Ships find it very useful to guide them to the port of Naples. Uracas is just like it.'

Again, a few days later, Dr Dan announced that the ship was sailing over a sunken island.

'It was called Victoria Island,' he said, 'in honour of Queen Victoria. It became part of the British Empire. A man named Marsters landed on the island with a gang of men to gather guano, bird droppings, valuable as fertilizer. They went away with a heavily loaded ship. A year later they came back but they couldn't find their island. They sailed right over the position of the island as we are doing now. They thought something must be the matter with their reckoning, so they searched the sea in every direction for a hundred miles. It was no use. Mr Marsters was very sad about it because the guano on that island was worth thousands of pounds. Perhaps some day it will come up again and the first man to get there may make a fortune.'

'I'd like to go down and take a look at a sunken island,' said Hal.

'Well, that's just what we're going to do tomorrow morning, when we get to Jack-in-the-Box.'

'Why do they call it Jack-in-the-Box?'

'Because it pops up and down. Its proper name is Falcon Island because it was discovered by the British warship *Falcon* in 1865. A lively volcano kept spouting lava and rocks until it had formed an island three miles long. Since it was near the Tonga Islands the King of Tonga claimed it and the Tongans danced all night in honour of the new island that the god of the sea had given them. Soon after that it disappeared.'

'That must have made the Tongans pretty sore.'

'It did. They held a scolding party and they all scolded the sea god. That didn't bring back their island. So they made a doll to look like the sea god and they poked it with spears and burned its fingers and toes. They thought if they tortured the sea god enough he would give them back their island. It didn't work. Then they decided to be nice to the sea god and perhaps he would be nice to them. They went to the shore and sang songs telling the sea god what a good fellow he was. They threw their best food into the sea for the god.

'Perhaps the way to a god's heart is through his stomach. Anyway in 1928 the submarine volcano began to spout and up came the island again. Once more the Queen claimed it and the Tongans cele-brated. The sea god was generous this time and kept piling up the island until it was six hundred feet high.

'But ten years later in spite of all the food they could throw into the sea and all their prayers and songs, the island disappeared.

'So you can see why ship captains call it Jack-in-the-Box.'

'Do you think it's going to pop up again?' asked Hal.

'That's what I want to find out. Ships have been reporting disturbances in the sea at that point. Tomorrow we'll go down and take a look.'

The prospect of exploring a submarine volcano was enough to get the boys up early the next morning. When they came on deck they found the ship had already heaved to. She lay softly rising and falling on a quiet sea.

'Jack-in-the-Box should be directly under us,' said Dr Dan. 'Listen.'

A deep rumbling sound could be heard. Then a geyser of steam shot up from the sea not far from the ship.

An unnaturally bright look always came into Dr Dan's eyes when he was close to danger and he was in the habit of pressing his hand against his left temple, as if in sudden pain. Hal saw these signs now, and they worried him.

At some time in the past something had happened that had been a severe blow to this man's nervous system. For anyone in such a condition, diving was dangerous. Even for a normal person it was hard on the nerves. Hal thought back to his own exciting experiences underwater. How much did the doctor really know about diving?

'Have you done much diving, Dr Dan?' Hal asked.

'Some.'

It wasn't a very satisfactory answer. Hal tried again. 'Have you used the aqualung?'

'Yes.'

'How often?'

Dr Dan showed some annoyance. 'What is this – a cross-examination?'

'I'm sorry,' Hal said. 'I meant no offence. You see, we had some pretty stiff times when we were diving for the Oceanographic. I think it scared me a little.'

'You don't need to go down if you don't want to.'

'It's not that,' Hal said. 'I just wondered – about you.'

'Well, for your information,' Dr Dan said with some heat, 'I've used an aqualung just once and that was in a swimming pool. My business has taken me up volcanoes, not down into the sea. But I understand that diving with an aqualung is very simple and I'm quite willing to try it. If you and Roger want to stay on deck, that's up to you.'

The taunt made Hal flush. He struggled to keep his temper.

'I was hoping,' he said, 'you would let us go down and you stay on deck. You could tell us just what to look for. We would bring back a report.'

'And just why should you go down and not I?' Dr Dan was becoming more and more angry.

'It's only that – that—' Hal stumbled. 'Well – it takes a good deal out of you. It's hard on the nerves.'

'But why should it be any harder on me than on you? What are you getting at?'

Hal had gone too far to be able to go back. 'When we were at Asama,' he said, 'walking along the edge of the crater – you didn't seem quite well. I mean – you stopped and stood for a couple of minutes as if you didn't know what was going on.'

Dr Dan laughed. 'Your imagination is running away with you. I'm not surprised – a volcano often has that effect upon a person who has never seen one before. The sight of it and the sound of it are enough to make you think crazy things. That's what happened to you.'

'Then,' persisted Hal, 'that night in the inn when the earthquake came you jumped up screaming, and beat on the wall like a madman.'

Dr Dan stared and his breathing came quick and hard. 'I don't know what's got into you, Hunt. Why you should make up these wild stories is beyond me. Next you'll be reporting to the American Museum that I'm not in my right mind and you'll try to take over my job. You have a lot of conceit. You've seen six volcanoes and already you think you know more about volcanoes than I do.'

'Not about volcanoes,' Hal said. 'But about diving. Have you ever heard of drunkenness of the deeps?'

'No, I have not, and I don't see what that has to do with it.'

'Divers sometimes get it. The pressure of the water packs too much nitrogen into the body tissues. I believe carbon dioxide has something to do with it, too. Anyhow, you get dreamy and woozy. You feel drunk. You forget where you are, you think you're in heaven, or walking on a cloud. You're apt to drop the air intake from your mouth and without any air you're done for.'

'But thousands of aqualungers go down without getting this – drunkenness of the deeps.'

'Yes, but it's always possible. It has a good deal to do with the nervous system. It's more likely to happen to a person if his nerves are – well – a bit on edge.'

The angry doctor forced himself to smile. 'Hal, the very fact that I haven't punched you on the nose for all this stuff and nonsense is sufficient evidence that my nerves are not on edge. Now, let's not waste any more time. Fetch up the aqualungs and let's get moving.'

Hal shrugged his shoulders and went below. The doctor looked after him with a puzzled frown on his face.

The gear was brought up from the hold. Hal and Dr Dan checked the equipment. The aqualung tanks were tested to make sure that they were full of compressed air.

Hal, Roger and the doctor got into their swimming trunks. They slipped their feet into rubber fins that flapped like a duck's feet as they walked over the deck. They put on belts loaded with one-pound chunks of lead. These weights were to counteract the lift of the water. Without them they would not be able to sink. Each of the two older men belted himself with five pounds of lead, but Roger took only four – since, strangely enough, the lighter a man is the less it takes to make him sink.

Then each man spat into his mask, rubbed the spittle over the glass, and rinsed it off in sea water. This would prevent the glass from fogging. Then the mask was strapped to the head. It covered the eyes and nose. From now on all breathing would have to be done through the mouth.

Each aqualung was put in place on a man's back

and strapped tight. Now they looked like men from Mars. The short air-hose was looped over the head and the mouthpiece placed in the mouth.

They practised breathing. The air came hard at first and the doctor's face grew a bit purple. A few sharp breaths, and the air began to flow easily.

The young doctor led the way to the gunwale and climbed over. The three let themselves down into the sea. They sank a few feet, then hung suspended.

They were in a pale green world. The surface of the water above them looked like a silken veil being waved gently by the breeze. Down through it came dancing, wavering shafts of sunlight. At one side was the dark shape of the *Lively Lady's* hull.

Small fish swam up and looked them over curiously, opening and closing their mouths. They seemed to be saying, 'Oh, Mabel, look at these funny things! This is something to write home about!'

One of them came close enough to nibble Roger's toe. He kicked and they all fled – but soon came back, ohing and ahing as before.

The water was quite warm. That would be because of the fires beneath. There was a constant rumbling and every once in a while came a sharp jolt that shook the sea and started queer currents coming and going.

The doctor seemed content to stay put for a moment, practising his breathing. Hal stayed near by. He was determined not to let the doctor out of his sight. Roger had already started swimming downwards. He was used to diving but, being adventurous, he was apt to take chances that might get him into trouble. Hal wondered how he was going to keep watch over both of his companions, the one too inexperienced, the other too venturesome.

At last Dr Dan began to swim down and Hal followed. Bubbles rose in streams from the exhaust valves of their aqualungs. Small fish rushed at the bubbles, thinking they were something to eat.

Hal began to feel the pressure on his eardrums. He remembered learning that water pressure is doubled at a depth of thirty-three feet. The mask began to press too tightly against his face. He exhaled a little through his nose into the mask. That was the way you increased the air pressure inside the mask against the water pressure outside. On the other hand, if the mask was a bit loose and began to leak, you inhaled through the nose in order to bring it more tightly against the face.

He wished that he had thought to tell Dr Dan about these tricks. But then the doctor might have thought he was just trying to show off his superior knowledge. It was hard to give advice to your boss.

Now it was possible to see the bottom. But it was the strangest sea bottom that Hal had ever looked upon.

It was a crater, very much like the craters he had seen on land, though smaller. He could not see clear to the other side of it but, from the curve, he judged it to be about five hundred yards in diameter. The inside slopes were very steep and descended to mysterious depths where the water became almost black, shot through with rays of firelight.

At every explosion the blackness would suddenly disappear in a blaze of lights that hurt the eyes and underwater billows would be set up that beat the bodies of the divers back and forth.

Hal, floating over the crater, felt like an aviator in a balloon or helicopter looking down into a live volcano. No burning breath came up from this volcano, but the water was quite hot. Large bubbles of gas rose. These did not bother the divers for they were breathing the pure air from their aqualungs. Yellow streaks in the water were probably sulphur.

Dr Dan deliberately swam down into the crater. Hal came close behind. He could not see Roger anywhere. Where was that young fool?

This was a new sensation, actually inside a crater, but floating just out of reach of its fiery claws. The only trouble was the heat – it was getting hard to bear. A little more of this and the fish would have boiled humans for supper.

Now the bottom of the crater could be seen. It was a bubbling pond of red lava, burning fiercely in spite of the chilling ocean, tumbling and leaping and sometimes exploding to throw up fountains of fire and rocks. This vision of a submarine volcano would remain with Hal all his life.

It was too hot for comfort. Hal was relieved to see Dr Dan turn and swim upwards. They reached the edge of the crater and stopped to rest. Still there was nothing to be seen of Roger, and Hal grew more anxious.

Suddenly a major explosion shook the volcano and up came a geyser of lava and stones, tearing along at great speed with a ripping, sizzling sound, and finally bursting into the air above and falling in a heavy shower. Hal was thankful that they had not been in its path. Down came the rocks and chunks of lava through the water to settle on the slopes of the volcano. They had lost their red heat but were still hot to the touch.

If this sort of thing continued – if more and more material were thrown up and deposited on the slopes of the volcano, the island of Jack-in-the-Box would rise again from the sea. Then the Tongans could have another party; and the hydrographers would have to put the island back on their charts.

There was that young rascal at last. Hal could see Roger coming through the blue. Roger caught sight of him at the same instant and finned his way towards him, excitedly waving his hands and pointing down the outside slope of the volcano.

He landed between Hal and Dr Dan and tugged at their arms, then swam away, looking back to see if they were following.

Evidently the kid had found something. Hal and

the doctor swam after him. The sea grew darker as they went deeper. Presently they made out through the gloom a mysterious form. It was not rock and it was not waving kelp.

It was a house. Near it were other houses. In fact, here was a whole village beneath the sea.

Dr Dan was delighted. Roger had put his time to good use and discovered something very interesting. The doctor walked about, each springy step taking him ten feet or more because of the buoyancy of the water.

The houses were built of lava blocks with wooden rafters so firmly embedded in the blocks that they had not floated away. The thatch that had once covered the rafters had disappeared.

Dr Dan was quite excited by this discovery and went from house to house examining the method of construction and picking up small articles that had been left by the people who had once lived here. He began to go into one house but leaped back when the arm of a large octopus licked out towards him.

He turned towards Hal and laughed excitedly, almost dropping the air intake from his mouth. Hal could see his eyes bright and hard within the mask.

The doctor began to wave his hands about in happy fashion, like a child.

Hal's worst fears were realized. The doctor had that strange underwater malady that was variously called 'drunkenness of the deeps', 'sea intoxication', 'rapture of the depths', 'nitrogen narcosis', or 'diver's sleep'.

Whatever you chose to call it, it was bad. He must get the doctor to the surface at once.

Hal pointed upwards and began to swim. But the doctor did not follow. Hal went back and took his arm and tried to swim up with him. Dr Dan fought him off and his eyes blazed with indignation.

Hal beckoned to Roger. The boy was quick to realize that something was wrong with the doctor. He took one arm and Hal the other and they started up.

Dr Dan furiously wrenched himself loose. Then he went dancing away among the houses. Each push on the ground sent him bounding up several feet high. This delighted him. He made higher and higher jumps.

A house barred his path. He made a mighty leap, soared twenty feet up into space and came down upon the ridgepole. He laughed again but the air intake luckily remained in his mouth. He walked along the ridge-pole as if it were a tightrope. Reaching the end of it, he leaped to the roof of another house.

Hal signalled to Roger and they swam up to the depths-crazed doctor. Hal again pointed upwards, smiled at the doctor, tried to quieten him.

But when he ventured to put his hand on Dr Dan's arm a wild look came over the doctor's face and he swung out with both fists. Hal got one in the face and Roger one in the stomach. Fortunately the water cushioned the blows.

When they recovered from their surprise the doctor was gone. He went prancing off over the rooftops, as happy as a colt in a field of clover. Hal and Roger swam swiftly after him.

If the doctor should slip on a rafter and fall into a house he might very well drop into the arms of a hungry octopus. It was just such black holes as these that the octopus loved.

A shadow passed above and Hal looked up to see a lazy shark watching with great interest the antics of these strange humans. Then another shark moved in. Hal felt that he and his companions were becoming too popular.

Dr Dan came slowly walking towards Hal. He stopped and cupped his hand behind his ear as if he were listening. A dreamy smile lay on his face. It is common for one suffering from rapture of the depths to think that he hears lovely music, a great orchestra, or a heavenly choir.

Dr Dan raised his eyes and saw the sharks. They appeared to interest him but he did not seem to realize what they were. He swam up towards them and Hal was not quick enough to stop him.

The doctor came close under the bigger shark. Then with all his force he punched its white belly.

If he had done this to a tiger shark or a white shark he would not have lived to regret it. Luckily this was a sand shark and although he was huge he was also a bit timid. He contented himself with switching his tail and swimming off.

The swing of the big tail caught the doctor on the side of the head, knocked off his mask and dislodged the air intake from his mouth. He began to sink slowly like a limp rag. Evidently the blow had knocked him unconscious. Without air, he would very quickly drown. Blood trickled from his forehead.

Hal and Roger already had him in their grip and

were forcing him up towards the surface.

The other shark came nearer, attracted by the smell of blood. Hal could see it more clearly now and realized with a shock that this one was no sand shark. It was a mako, often called the man-eater because it does not hesitate to attack divers.

Hal and Roger thrashed the water in a vain attempt to frighten it away. At last they broke the surface and looked about for the ship. It lay a good five hundred yards distant. They could easily lose a leg or two to the mako if they tried to swim that far.

Hal dropped the intake from his mouth and shouted. The quick ear of Omo heard him and the Polynesian boy came running to the forepeak.

'Bring the boat,' shouted Hal. 'Shark!'

Omo flung off the painter of the boat that lay on the water alongside the ship, jumped in and rowed with all his might. Hal and Roger faced the shark and beat the water with the palms of their hands. They knew it was hard to scare a man-eater, but they could only try.

The shark edged closer. Its ugly face appeared above the surface, then sank again. The boys shouted and slapped and were glad that Omo's arms were strong.

The small boat came zipping over the water with the speed of a flying-fish. It seemed to worry the man-eater, and he hesitated to strike. He had just about made up his mind to it when the boat arrived and stopped with a savage back-churning of the oars.

'What happened to Dr Dan?' cried Omo as he hauled the limp form of the doctor into the boat. The others climbed in and they set out for the ship.

'He went drunk,' said Hal. 'Then he lost his air.'

In a few moments the doctor was on the ship's deck and was being manipulated to get the sea water out of him. After this was done, he lay unconscious for a good five minutes.

'He'll come out of it,' Hal said. 'His pulse is all right.'

At last the doctor's eyes fluttered open and he looked lazily about. He pressed his hand against his left temple. So he lay for several minutes, resting. Then he smiled at Hal, a rather bitter smile.

'Well, my boy, you see I didn't get the bends after all.'

'The bends?' said Hal. 'I said you might get drunkenness of the deeps.'

'Oh, is that something different?'

'Quite different.'

'Very well, then, I didn't get your drunkenness of the deeps.'

Evidently the doctor remembered nothing of what had happened during the last dreadful half hour.

'That was an interesting village,' he said. So he did remember the village.

'And an interesting shark,' put in Roger.

Dr Dan looked up at him inquiringly. 'There were no sharks, Roger. Perhaps you mistook some shadows for sharks.'

'There were sharks, Dr Dan,' Hal said. 'And you had a run-in with them. But you didn't know about it. You were drunk.'

Dr Dan looked at him a long time without answering. Then he sat up and began to unstrap the fins from his feet.

'Hal,' he said slowly, 'I don't know what your game is. Whatever it is, I don't like it. I thought you were a good sort. It seems I made a mistake.'

Roger came to his brother's defence. 'There really was a shark, Dr Dan.'

'I saw it, too,' Omo said.

Dr Dan looked up with a bitter smile. 'So you are all in the plot against me. That amounts to mutiny, doesn't it? Well, you won't get away with it. I may have to put up with you until we reach Hawaii – then what a pleasure it will be to get rid of you and your ship.'

12
The Eruption of Tin Can

The news came crackling over the air:

'Eruption at Niuafou.'

The *Lively Lady* trimmed her sails for Niuafou. 'Sailors call it Tin Can Island,' Captain Ike told the boys.

'Because the people get their food in tin cans?' guessed Roger.

'As a matter of fact, the people live on coconuts and fish. No, there's a stranger reason than that for calling it Tin Can Island. Ships carrying mail don't bother to go inshore. Natives swim out to get the mail. The ship's carpenter seals up all the mail in large biscuit tins. When these are thrown overboard they float because of the air in them and the swimmers push them ashore. Now they sometimes come out in a canoe because a shark got one of their swimmers.'

'I think I have some stamps from Tin Can Island in my stamp collection,' said Roger.

'Yes, stamp collectors are pretty keen to get them. They'd better get them while they can. Some day that old volcano is going to blow Tin Can Island right off the map.'

It was only two hundred miles from Jack-in-the-Box to Tin Can, less than a day's run for the *Lively Lady*.

The first thing to be seen was a pillar of smoke. Gradually the island beneath it came into view.

'I've been looking it up in my geology manual,' Dr Dan told Captain Ike, as the boys listened in. 'This island is really one big volcano. It stands on the bottom of the ocean six thousand feet down. That means that the volcano is more than a mile high, but only the rim of the crater projects above the surface. Inside the crater is a lake three miles wide. There's supposed to be a break in the rim if we can find it, we can sail into the lake. Let's try it.'

'Doesn't sound too good to me,' said Captain Ike doubtfully. 'Don't like the idea of sailing my ship straight into an exploding crater.'

'The lake isn't exploding. The eruption is coming from vents in the rim.'

'But the lake could blow up any time couldn't it?'

'I suppose it could. We have to take that chance. We're here to study this thing, and how are we going to study it unless we get close to it?'

Captain Ike grumbled and chewed on the stem of his pipe. The boys had gone up to the crow's-nest to get a better look at the strange crater-island.

Captain Ike lowered his voice. 'There's something I've been wanting to say to you, Dan Adams. If you know what's good for you, don't get yourself into tight spots. It makes your nerves go haywire.'

'That's ridiculous!' exploded Dr Dan. 'The boys have been filling your ears with wild stories. I must say I'm disappointed in those boys. They are tricky and underhanded, and the older one seems to have some idea of discrediting me so that I will be fired and he will get my job.'

'Now be reasonable, Doc. How could he get your job knowing so little about volcanoes?'

'That's just the point,' said Dr Dan. 'He doesn't know so little. He's seen quite a number of volcanoes by this time and he's been studying every book I have on board. I hate to give him credit for it but he has a sharp mind – he learns fast.'

'So you're afraid of him,' Captain Ike taunted. 'A boy not yet out of his teens!'

Dr Dan bristled. 'I'm not afraid of anybody. But I don't trust him, nor his brother, nor that Omo.'

'Do you trust me?'

Dr Dan shifted uneasily. 'You talk like the rest of them.'

Captain Ike chuckled. 'Put your mind at rest,' he said. 'Nobody wants to do you in. You've got the boys all wrong. I suppose you wouldn't believe me if I told you they saved your life when you went balmy during that dive.'

Dr Dan's cheeks paled and his eyes fixed upon Captain Ike grew hard and bright. 'That's their story,' he said. 'You weren't down there to see for yourself, were you? Yet you take the word of a couple of schoolboys against mine.'

Captain Ike could see that the doctor was getting dangerously angry.

'Skip it,' he said. 'Forget it. Where did you say that channel was?'

'Somewhere on this side. Probably over there at that low point.'

The doctor's guess proved to be correct. As they came closer, they could see the pass into the lake. It was a very narrow pass, not more than thirty feet wide, but the *Lively Lady* easily slipped through. Then the little ship found herself, for the first time in her life, actually inside a volcano.

All around rose the crater wall. In most places it was about six hundred feet high but on the northern side reached almost a thousand.

The boys had seen something like it before. It reminded them of Crater Lake in Oregon. There, too, a crater was filled with water, but it was a dead crater.

This was a live one. Only a few jets of steam rose from the lake itself. But on the western shore a row of small craters like chimneys sent up clouds of smoke and steam. They were the children of the great crater. Dr Dan counted them.

'Thirty craters in action,' he said.

That part of the rim was very savage and terrible. But the rest of the circular island was beautiful. It was heavily wooded with mangoes, coconuts, ironwood, pandanus and other tropical trees and shrubs. Peeping from the trees were native villages. The boys counted nine of them.

'It gets me,' said Captain Ike. 'All these people – living on the edge of a volcano.'

'Thirteen hundred people live here,' Dr Dan answered. 'There have been five bad eruptions in the last century – still they hang on. Not that I blame them much.' He looked about at the beautiful groves of trees and the cosy villages on top of the craterwall. 'A nice place to live so long as it doesn't blow up.'

Only one man on board had been here before. That was the brown young sailor, Omo, who had been born in the South Seas and lived there all his life. He had once visited Tin Can in a trading schooner.

He pointed to a village perched on the highest point of the north rim. 'That's the village of Angaha,' he said. 'The high chief of that village rules the whole island. Once some of his people rebelled and went to the south rim and built their own village. They refused to pay taxes to the high chief. Their headman declared he would rather have his village destroyed by the gods than pay taxes to the high chief. He had hardly said these words before the ground opened up under his own house and hot lava began to spurt out. It killed him and burned his house and flowed out through the village. It burned every house to the ground and killed sixty people.'

'And that was blamed on the gods,' Hal said.

'Yes. The gods get blamed for everything bad and thanked for everything good that happens. You see, the people don't understand the scientific reasons for these things. For instance, when there's an earthquake, they think it's caused by their god Maui. He is supposed to be sleeping far down in the earth and when he rolls over, that makes an earthquake.'

'He's rolling over now,' said Hal, as a violent shiver ran through the lake, making the *Lively Lady* dance. Landslides of rock and ash slid down the crater walls and splashed into the lake. Screams could be heard from the shore and Captain Ike, who was using the binoculars, reported, 'That tumbled down several houses. The people are running around like frightened ants.'

'I'm afraid they're in for a bad time,' Dr Dan said. 'Thirty craters all going at once can make a lot of trouble.'

Ashes and cinders were raining down upon the deck. Now and then a larger chunk arrived. Hal picked one up – it was not very hot and it was extremely light.

'It's pumice,' he said. 'Just like that big rock we found on Mt Asama.'

He tossed it into the water and it floated. Patches of pumice like little yellow islands bounced up and down on the ripples.

Another object struck the deck with a loud thud. Roger went to pick it up.

'Don't,' warned Hal. 'It's hot!'

'But the one you picked up wasn't hot.'

'I know, but it was pumice, full of air holes. That's one of the blocks - I've been reading about them. And that's a bomb,' he added as something burst with a loud report only ten feet above their heads and the fragments fell about them.

'Well, what's the difference between a block and a bomb?'

'A block is a piece of solid rock. A bomb is a block that is hollow inside and filled with gas. The gas explodes and blows the rock to bits.'

The god Maui rolled over again in his sleep. Avalanches thundered down into the lake. In the village of Angaha a stone church on the heights suddenly swayed, then dissolved, and fell flat. Showers of bombs were exploding over the houses, setting many of them on fire. The people were in a panic. Where could they go to escape the thirty monsters?

'They ought to be evacuated,' said Dr Dan. 'But it would take a bigger ship than ours to carry them off. We'd better send for help.'

He went below and dispatched a message summoning any ships within call to come at once to remove the inhabitants of Tin Can Island.

He got only one response. It was from a steamer by the name of *Matua*. Its captain reported that his ship's position was nearly two hundred miles from Tin Can and he could not promise to arrive before morning.

Blasts of fire shot up from the craters. At the same instant another violent earthquake shook the island and a great section of the ridge broke away and fell into the lake.

'I've had enough of this,' said Captain Ike. 'Like it or not, I'm taking the *Lady* out of this hell-hole.' He gave orders to Omo and the ship was smartly brought about and headed for the pass.

An unhappy surprise awaited the little ship. She arrived at the rim only to find that there was no pass. The earthquakes had tumbled millions of tons of rock down into the thirty-foot channel, filling it completely from one side to the other. Where there had been clear water there was now a wall of rock twenty feet high.

13
The Ship in the Volcano

'Now you've done it,' stormed Captain Ike, venting his anger on Dr Dan. 'Got us trapped in a live volcano. What'll you do about that?'

'Your guess is as good as mine,' admitted Dr Dan. 'We probably can't do anything until morning. Then perhaps we can land and cross the island and escape on the *Matua*.'

'And leave the *Lively Lady* here?' exclaimed Captain Ike. 'Not on your life! I'm not going to abandon this ship to be burned and sunk. If she stays, I stay. You got her in here – you'd better stir your volcanic brains to get her out of here because I'm not leaving until she does.'

The *Lively Lady* put about and sailed to the side of the lake farthest away from the thirty craters. Even here the shower of ashes, cinders, blocks and bombs was continuous and dangerous.

Terrified natives on top of the ridge signalled to the ship, but there was nothing the *Lively Lady* could do for them. Conversation was impossible at such a distance and the cliff was too steep at this point for anyone to climb up or down.

Every moment more houses burst into flame. Their thatch roofs and basket-like walls made them burn as easily as paper.

The sails of the *Lively Lady* were tight-furled and hoses were kept busy sprinkling her down and putting out the small fires that repeatedly burst forth in spite of all that could be done.

So far the great crater in which lay the lake had appeared to be dead, except for a few spurts of steam here and there. But now it began to show signs of fiery life. Three small islands in the lake, each with its own little crater, began to grumble and smoke.

They were little craters in comparison with the chief crater three miles wide, but Hal estimated that even the smallest of them was a thousand feet across. Soon the three island craters were bellowing like bulls and throwing up blazing volleys of blocks and bombs. The bombs exploded like cannon.

'Close your eyes,' Roger said, 'and you'd think it was a naval battle.'

'But you'd better not close your eyes,' said Hal, 'or you'll get a whack on the head.'

It was necessary to keep constant watch above to avoid the falling rocks. They could be seen long before they arrived. It was fairly easy to step out of their way at the last moment and let them whang into the deck.

Easy, unless they came a dozen or more close together and you couldn't get out of the way of one without getting into the way of another.

As night came on they glowed in the darkness and looked like fireballs dropping out of the sky. Hundreds of the bombs exploded in mid-air, flinging red-hot slivers in all directions. It was like a grand display of fireworks.

'Remember the fireworks we saw at the New York State Fair?' Roger said. 'It cost them two million dollars. And we get this for nothing.'

Hal laughed. 'Just born lucky, I guess,' and he jumped to dodge another block.

'You fellows had better get below,' said Captain Ike briskly as he passed with a bucket of water to put out a fire.

The boys seized the deck hose and helped him. When the blaze was out Hal said:

'You need us up here. Besides, we wouldn't want to miss the fun.'

Captain Ike growled. 'What fools you young-uns can be! So this is fun! When you get as old as me and have a ship to look after you won't think it's fun to get caught in a blowing-up volcano.'

'Guess you're right,' said Hal and began industriously hosing off the heavy load of ashes that lay on the deck.

Roger seized a shovel and went about looking for heavy chunks. While he searched, he kept the shovel over his head like a steel helmet – blocks whanged down upon it and bounded away. When he found blocks, bombs, pumice stones, or pasty blobs of hot lava, he shovelled them off into the water. Where he saw fire starting he called his brother, and Hal came running with the hose.

So they kept working feverishly for two hours to save the ship. Then they breathed more easily as the three island craters quietened and the shower of fire ceased. They began to hope that the eruption was dying down.

But old Tin Can was only drawing in his breath and getting ready to burst out with a new performance. The god of the underworld had failed to wipe out these human ants with one trick, so he would try another.

With a deafening roar the cliff above their heads split open and a jet of flame shot out. With it came strange greenish clouds that rolled and tumbled and then sank towards the ship.

'Gas,' said Dr Dan. 'I wonder what kinds.'

He began sniffing as eagerly as if he were smelling a fragrant rose. The gases had a very bad smell.

'Sulphur dioxide, ammonia, azote . . .' Dr Dan named them off. 'But the worst are the ones you can't see or smell – carbon dioxide and carbon monoxide.'

Everyone began to cough and choke. Soon they were gasping like fish out of water. It seemed to Hal as if a heavy blanket had been laid over his nose and mouth. He was suffocating.

At the same time a drowsy laziness was stealing through him. All he wanted to do was to lie down and sleep. It no longer seemed important to save the ship or to save himself. Nothing mattered any more.

He roused himself fiercely. He knew what was happening – the carbon gases were getting them down. But how could they escape them?

'Let's sail out into the lake,' he suggested. 'Perhaps it won't be so bad out there.'

'There's no wind,' objected Captain Ike. 'But I can use the engine.'

'Don't do that!' yelled Dr Dan, but he was too late.

Omo, who was as quick as a cat, had already jumped to the motor and pressed the starter. At once there was a deafening explosion and a blaze of flame and Omo was thrown ten feet across the deck. The motor conked out.

'Lucky that was just a small pocket of gas,' said Dr Dan. 'If it had been a big one it would have taken all of us and the ship too. Some of these gases are highly explosive. We can't use the motor.'

'Then we're stuck,' said Captain Ike, sitting down heavily on a hatch cover, pressing his hand against his dizzy head.

'Are there any gas masks on board?' Dr Dan asked.

Captain Ike snorted. 'Gas masks! Whoever heard of a ship carrying gas masks?'

He relaxed and lay down on the hatch cover. That seemed a sensible thing to do. Everyone felt the same way – why not give up and relax?

'Gas masks,' Hal mumbled dreamily. Then a sudden thought stirred him awake. 'Gas masks! Why of course we have gas masks, or something just as good. The aqualungs!'

They stared at each other, trying to clear their brains. Along with the suffocating gas had come intense heat and the perspiration rolled down their faces. It was hard to think. The idea began to penetrate. The aqualungs – yes, why not?

They got unsteadily to their feet and hurried as fast as their wobbly legs would take them down the companionway to get the aqualungs. They brought them to the deck and put them on. When the mouthpieces were in place they began to breathe the sweet and blessed air from the tanks.

It was like gradually coming out of some horrible dream. The mists that had clouded their brains slowly cleared. In the light of the burning houses far above they could see each other's faces becoming less tight and drawn and the drooping eyes opening with new hope. Life began to seem rather important after all.

But were they to be free of the gas only to be baked in the heat? The sweat rolled down their bodies as the temperature steadily climbed higher and higher. Out of the vent in the cliff came the breath of fires twenty miles down, fires hot enough to make iron run like molasses.

Hal leaned heavily upon the rail and looked down into the black water. It had never looked more cool and inviting. If he could only bury himself in it! It was pretty sad to be so close to coolness and yet perish of the heat.

Bury himself in it – why not? Why hadn't he thought of it before?

The others were astonished to see him suddenly break into a laugh and beckon them to the rail and point downwards. Then, without bothering to undress, he climbed over the rail and let himself down into the water.

At any other time it would have seemed warm, for, although the fires were not directly beneath it, its temperature had been raised a little by the hot objects that had fallen into it. But to Hal in his superheated condition it seemed delightfully cool. He felt new life flowing through his parched body.

He waited anxiously for the others to join him, hoping they would not be overcome by the heat before they could enjoy this delicious relief. They were soon with him and floated about with their heads above water, broad smiles on their faces.

But the heat on their heads was still terrific and they presently sought refuge beneath the surface. Down they went, ten feet deep to escape the warmer surface water. There they hung, breathing easily, comfort and coolness stealing into their bones.

Above them was a red glow and at one side was the black shadow of the hull of the *Lively Lady*. Fish swam over their heads making black silhouettes against the gleam of the fires. They could only hope that the fish would all be small and friendly. Hal thought of the shark that had taken the mail swimmer.

Perhaps there were no sharks in the lagoon. On the other hand, there might be more sharks here than outside because the refuse from the villages was probably thrown into the lake.

But he felt it would be more pleasant to be nibbled by a shark than slowly roasted to death by volcanic heat.

A greater shadow now lay overhead, shutting out the glow. It was too broad to be a shark, and too still. What would be that broad? A moon fish would be only four or five feet wide – this was much wider.

It could be a sea bat or manta ray, that great pancake

of a fish that measures ten feet or more across. Hal looked for the long whip tail that could cut like a knife, but could not see it.

Roger had also noticed the thing and decided to find out what it was. Before Hal could stop him he swam up and poked his fist into the black object. All he got for his pains were a few bruised knuckles but the black thing did not move.

Hal and Dr Dan joined in the investigation. Touching the bottom of the mass, they swam out until they reached its edge. Then they raised their heads above water and found that the thing was a small island of pumice, the rock that floats. The pumice blocks were piled almost three feet high.

Roger, who could never let well enough alone, gleefully clambered up on to the island.

'This is something to tell them when I get home,' he crowed. 'Afloat on a raft made of rock.'

Then the raft suddenly gave way beneath him and he dropped through the hole into the water, scratching himself plentifully on the sharp-edged rocks as he passed.

Hal and Dr Dan also retreated again underwater, for the heat above was still intense.

How long would they have to stay below? The air in the aqualungs would last for only one hour. Then they would have no choice. They must come up, or drown.

Their watery prison seemed to be growing darker and darker. Hal hoped this meant that the fires above were dying down. But he was afraid that this explanation was too simple. He suspected a different reason for the growing darkness – more pumice was drifting in to cover the surface. A rock roof was forming over their heads that might become so thick and so broad that their escape would be cut off.

They would be like the divers he had heard of who had gone down in arctic waters to explore a wreck that lay on the bottom. The ice floes closed in over their heads and they never came up. This situation would be the same except that the roof would be rock instead of ice.

He could see Dr Dan looking up and knew that the scientist was also aware of the growing danger. Would it excite him, cause him to do wild things, or freeze him in one of his strange trances? Then the air intake would drop from his mouth and he would be finished.

Hal thought of the bitter and untrue things the doctor had said of him. He had practically called him a coward and a sneak. If it had been anybody else, thought Hal, he would have given him a sound thrashing. But he couldn't thrash a sick man. There was nothing for Hal to do but to swallow his resentment and play nurse to this crackpot, and hope that some day whatever was wrong in that brilliant brain would be corrected.

When Hal judged that three-quarters of an hour had passed he went up to investigate. He had to search for several minutes before he could find a hole in the pumice. He thrust out his head.

The flame spouting from the fissure in the cliff was no longer white-hot, only red-hot. The heat that lay on the water was less terrific than before, but still too much for a human body to bear. Hal felt his head steaming as if it had been poked into an oven and his eyes began to ache.

He dropped again below the surface and saw the light above him fade as the pumice closed in and filled the hole.

He could not see a thing. He could only hope that the others were still near by. He groped about in the

dark, hoping to lay his hands upon Roger, Dr Dan, anybody.

At last he got hold of something cool and smooth but it jumped away from him with such speed that he concluded it must be a surprised fish.

Then his hand closed upon someone's wrist. It was a fairly small wrist and might be Roger's – he hoped so.

Keeping his grip, he continued the search with his free hand. Finally, he clutched a trembling something that might be the tentacle of a giant octopus – no, it was a human arm, and it would hardly be Captain Ike's or Omo's for he could not conceive of any power on earth making those hard-bitten sailors tremble. It must be Dr Dan, and his nerves had begun to slip. The arm jerked once or twice but Hal held on.

Just a few minutes now and everything would be decided, for better or worse.

It happened sooner than he expected. His air died down, failed completely, and he found himself sucking a vacuum. He took his hand way from Roger long enough to turn the little lever on his tank that switched on the five-minute reserve.

He felt for Roger's lever to see if the boy had turned

it on – he had. Then he explored to see if the doctor had done the same – he had not. Hal twisted the lever so that new air would rush into the scientist's lungs.

He felt other hands now, probably Omo's and Captain Ike's. It was good that they were all together. They must stand by each other. They had only five minutes now before the reserve air would fail – five minutes to escape from their underwater tomb.

Hal rose towards the surface, drawing the others with him. He had laid his plans. It would do no good to go hunting for holes. There might not be a hole for hundreds of yards and the chances of their finding it were very slim.

If they scattered and went in different directions one or two of them might find holes but the rest would perish. They must stay together and work together.

He rose until his head grazed the pumice roof.

He took the block his head had touched, drew it down into the water, and pressed it into Roger's hands. Then he gave Roger a push.

The boy guessed his brother's plan. The blocks were to be removed one by one to make a hole in the roof. Each block must be taken several yards away before it was released or it would simply pop back into the hole. Roger left his rock at a safe distance and came back for another. In the meantime Hal had been initiating the others. Dr Dan joined him in plucking chunks from overhead and passing them to Roger, Omo and Captain Ike who carried them away.

Presently a light broke through; after the removal of a few more blocks there was a man-sized hole.

Then Hal seized Roger and in spite of that young gentleman's efforts to make somebody else go first he was pushed up through the hole. He scrambled out on the roof. He reached down and helped the next man up – Dr Dan.

The doctor noticed that the hole was beginning to close again. He worked above to keep it open while the men below removed more blocks. Then up came Omo, Captain Ike and, finally, Hal. The last man was hardly out before the opening closed again.

The men breathed the last of the tank air, then dropped the intakes from their mouths. The evil gases had thinned and the heat was no longer intolerable.

The next thing was to get to the ship. It lay fifty yards away. That did not seem far; but moving over the roof was more of a job than it appeared to be. Although the blocks were wedged tightly together and, in some cases, lightly cemented to each other by the heat, it was unsafe to trust one's full weight on any one spot. Also the roof was thicker in some places than in others.

So they went along on all fours, sometimes even lying flat, the better to distribute their weight, and inching forward as if on thin ice. At one time Dr Dan's foot went through and he would have followed it if Captain Ike and Omo had not been close enough to pull him out. After this incident the doctor lay for a moment, breathing hard. But he pulled himself together and the crawl to the ship continued.

Only when they were all safely aboard did he let go completely. In the middle of a sentence he dropped to the deck and was at once sound asleep – or had he fainted? Hal could not be sure which.

Just to make certain that the man had not died of heart attack Hal felt for the pulse. The fact that it was going like a power hammer indicated that the doctor was far from dead.

'Let's get him into his bunk,' Hal said.

Omo unstrapped the aqualung and he and Hal

carried the limp figure down to the cabin. They stripped off the wet clothes, towelled down the body, and tucked the doctor still sound asleep into his bunk.

Hal and Roger were glad to crawl into their own bunks for a few hours' sleep. Omo curled up on the open deck for a nap, ready to jump into action at any moment.

14
Saint Elmo's Fire

Captain Ike was too anxious about his ship to take rest. He strode up and down the deck muttering and grumbling, watching the spurts of flame from the cliff, the firelight of burning villages, the blazing fountains that shot up irregularly from the thirty craters.

Above all he watched the weather. His seaman's nose told him that the huge cloud of steam, smoke and gas that shut out the sky was very much like the clouds that announce a hurricane. Not knowing much about volcanoes, he couldn't be sure, but he didn't trust those rolling, tumbling masses that seemed to be fighting battles with each other as they were carried here and there by contradictory air currents.

Forked lightning leaped back and forth, as if the giants of the upper air were making war upon each other with huge yellow spears. In other parts of the cloud there was a different kind of lightning that came in sudden sheets instead of spears. It was as if someone were hanging out washing on the clothes lines of heaven and then suddenly snatching it away again.

189

'I don't like it, I don't like it, I don't like it.' Each time Captain Ike put his foot down he said, 'I don't like it.'

Then he stopped in amazement and looked up at the masts. They were glowing like the illuminated hands of a watch. A shimmering ghostly light bathed them from top to bottom. Even the rigging was all lined with light.

'A good sign!' cried Captain Ike.

Omo started up. 'Did you call?'

'No, lad. But look what we got here. Ghosts have come aboard.'

'That is very bad,' said Omo. 'Our people believe those are the spirits of the dead. Something very bad will happen.'

'Nonsense. Don't you know what this is? It's St Elmo's Fire. St Elmo protects sailors. This is a sign he's looking after us. We're going to get out of here okay.'

'Isn't that just a white man's superstition?'

'White men don't have superstitions. It's just you browns who have the superstitions.'

But he had no sooner said it than doubt struck him. How could he say that the brown man's notions were any more foolish than the white man's? He had known some pretty silly whites and some very sensible Polynesians.

'Oh well, perhaps we're both wrong,' he admitted. 'The science fellows say it ain't ghosts at all, just electricity. Look at that!'

An orange-coloured star glowed just above the point of the foremast. Captain Ike stared. 'Spooky, ain't it? Some say it's the Star of Bethlehem that will lead us safe.'

'But our people say . . .'

'There we go again,' laughed Captain Ike. 'It never happens except when there's lightning so it's probably electric, as they say. And there's a blue star perched on the mainmast. The orange, they tell me, is a positive discharge and the blue is negative. Listen to it!'

A distinct hissing or crackling sound came from the illuminated masts and rigging. It grew louder when lighting flashed overhead and died away whenever the sky went dark. For more than an hour the orange and blue blurs of light, vaguely star-shaped, burned above the mastheads. Then they disappeared as a heavy fall of rain hit the ship.

With the rain came wind, wild blundering wind that

seemed to come in circles rather than in straight lines. The ship was anchored fore and aft but the anchors began to drag. Now it seemed that the *Lively Lady* would be carried against the rocky slope of one of the small islands, and now that she would be dashed into the cliff.

Hal and Roger came tumbling up, but there was little that anyone could do. Man was weak and small indeed in the grip of the volcanic storm. Dr Dan, if he had been awake, might have told the why of what was going on, but could have done nothing to prevent it.

The crater lake began to twist and bounce under the wind and the floating pumice scraped up and down on the ship's hull. At every grind and scratch, Captain Ike winced.

'Won't be a speck of paint left on her!' he lamented. 'We'll be lucky if it doesn't scrape a hole in her hull.'

The heat was now a thing of the past. The men, soaked to the skin, were chilled by the rain and wind.

And still there was heat, plenty of it, where the craters tossed up their fire into the face of the rain and the houses burned in spite of the downpour. Frequent earthquakes rumbled, starting avalanches on the cliffs and opening new cracks and fissures.

At dawn the storm abated but the earthquakes continued. After each one there could be heard several loud explosions that did not seem to come from the quakes themselves nor from the craters. Evidently they woke Dr Dan, who came on deck at sunrise.

'Those big bangs – what are they?' asked Captain Ike.

'Steam explosions,' Dr Dan said. 'Those quakes open up big cracks in the earth. If the cracks are under water, the water rushes down into them and strikes the hot lava. There it is changed into steam and that makes an explosion.'

Omo brought some hot food from the galley. The tropic sun began to dry out the wet clothes and warm the chilled bodies.

But there was small comfort in the fact that they were still trapped within a live volcano. They might save themselves by landing where the cliffs were low and crossing the island to the outer beach where they could be taken aboard the *Matua*.

But how about the *Lively Lady*? 'I won't leave her,' insisted Captain Ike. Nor did anyone else want to leave her. Their ship had become a trusted and loyal friend and they would not abandon her. But how could you ride a ship over a wall twenty feet high?

'Let's up anchor and take a look at that channel,' said Captain Ike. 'It may be open now.'

There was no reason why it should be open and it wasn't.

After the ship had ploughed slowly and heavily through the drifting pumice, the path that led to the ocean was found to be still choked with rock. They gazed at it helplessly.

'If we only had some dynamite,' mourned the unhappy captain.

'Dynamite,' repeated the others. At that moment dynamite seemed the most precious thing in the world. But there wasn't so much as a firecracker on board, let alone a stick of dynamite.

At one side of the pass a few feet above the water's edge was a crack in the rock. Smoke was coming from it.

'One of the quakes must have done that,' the doctor said.

They all stared dully at the smoke rising from the crack.

Then Hal's weary mind began to turn over, very unwillingly, like a cat that doesn't want to be disturbed. A crack. Smoke. Smoke meant fire. It must be very hot down in there.

He turned to Dr Dan. 'What were you saying about steam explosions?'

'Just that when water gets into a crack and strikes hot lava it makes steam and you get an explosion.'

'Enough of an explosion to blow that rock out of the pass?'

'It would probably do a lot more than that,' said Dr Dan. 'What are you getting at?'

Hal hesitated. 'It's a crazy idea. Probably it wouldn't work.'

Dr Dan said sarcastically, 'Then why waste our time with it?'

But the others were not so easily satisfied. Captain Ike demanded:

'What's on your mind, lad?'

'Well, I was just thinking, if water down that crack would make an explosion, why don't we put water down the crack?'

'How could we do it?'

'With the deck hose.'

Roger began to dance. 'Oh boy! That would blow the rock out of the pass and we could get out. Let's go!'

'Hold on,' said Hal. 'It's not so simple. It might blow out the rock – but at the same time it would blow us to Kingdom Come.'

Gloom settled once more upon the group. It had seemed a brilliant plan and for a moment they had imagined themselves safely outside the murderous volcano. Now once again they were hopeless prisoners.

Dr Dan's forehead was furrowed in thought. 'I'm not so sure the plan wouldn't work,' he said.

'But we have to bring the ship alongside to get the hose into the crack,' said Hal. 'An explosion would blast us to bits.'

'Not necessarily. The explosion wouldn't be immediate. It takes a little time for steam to form. If you set a kettle of water on a hot fire does it begin to steam right away?'

'No, it may take ten or fifteen minutes.'

'Exactly. Of course this fire is hotter than the fire in a stove. But we'll balance that by putting in a lot more water than you could get into a kettle, or a thousand kettles. If we pump a ton or two of water into that crack it ought to take ten or fifteen minutes for it to generate enough steam to make an explosion. We'll have time to haul off to a safe distance. I think you have something, Hunt,' he acknowledged with a bitter smile. 'I wish it had been my plan instead of yours, but I'm willing to go along with anything that will get us out of here.'

But Hal had another objection to his own plan. 'The crack,' he said. 'It will act like a safety valve. The steam will escape through the crack and there won't be any explosion.'

'Oh yes there will. How do you suppose all these other explosions occur? An earthquake makes a crack, water rushes in and makes steam that causes an explosion, in spite of the fact that some of the steam escapes through the crack. The point is that the crack is too small – it lets out only a tiny fraction of the steam. Think of a steam locomotive – you may see steam escaping from the valves but still there is enough to drive the pistons and pull a train a mile long. You see, the magic of steam is expansion. When water turns into steam it expands and must have sixteen hundred times as much space as when it was in the form of water. That means that enough water to fill a box four feet wide would change into a mass of steam as big as a house. That little two-inch crack won't let out enough of it to matter. I think we'll have an explosion, and a good one. Let's try it.'

15
Escape of the Lively Lady

It was amusing to see how the doctor went to work to carry out the plan of the man he disliked so heartily. Hal thought it showed that Dr Dan, though a bit sick in the head, was still a good sport.

With Omo at the engine and Captain Ike at the wheel the ship was brought close alongside the rocks. Hal and Dr Dan climbed ashore with the hose and Roger, determined not to miss anything, came after them.

The ground was hot underfoot. The crack was only a foot or so long and just wide enough to admit the nozzle of the two-inch hose.

The three men peered down into the fiery chamber. It opened out below into a cave that seemed to extend towards or beneath the pass and was brilliantly illuminated by the glow of white-hot lava.

They could look more than fifty feet down but still could not see the bottom. It was this tremendous chamber of fire that they were going to turn into a gigantic steam boiler. Fooling around on top of a steam boiler was nervous work. They could only hope the doctor was right and the thing would not pop as soon as the water struck the lava.

Hal signalled to Omo to start the pump. Water from the lake poured up through the hose and thundered down into the white cavern. It struck the blazing lava with the wild sizzling roar of cold against hot and immediately a cloud of steam rose. Was the thing going to blow up after all without giving them time to escape?

But as the deluge continued the pocket where the water landed turned from white to a dull red and the steam diminished. The cold water was being rapidly heated but more water kept tumbling in to delay the process. For five minutes the flood continued. Then Dr Dan shouted:

'That's enough!'

Omo turned off the pump. At the same moment he threw the idling engine into reverse. The ship was already moving backwards when the men scrambled aboard. The engine spluttered – everyone looked anxiously at Omo. It would be most unpleasant if the motor should fail now and leave them to be the victims of their own plans.

The engine coughed and spat, but it was only teasing. It did not really mean to let them down. Perhaps it loved the *Lively Lady* as much as they did. While threatening at any moment to go dead, it managed to keep turning and steadily drew the little ship back out of danger.

Dr Dan was not satisfied until they were half a mile away and close to one of the small islands. There the *Lively Lady* came to and the men gathered at the bow to await anxiously the result of their experiment.

The lazy plume of smoke issuing from the crack had been replaced by a strong, erect jet of steam. It was very slender but it shot up to a height of twenty or thirty feet.

'We could have plugged that hole,' said Roger.

'It wouldn't have done any good,' Dr Dan said. 'The steam would have blown the plug out.'

The hiss of the escaping steam could be plainly heard across the water. Then the column of steam suddenly enlarged to twice its former size.

'That means it has torn away some of the rock and made the hole bigger,' said Hal. 'If it keeps on doing that . . .'

But Dr Dan was not disturbed. He knew the

mechanics of steam. 'It's like this,' he said. 'Suppose there's a giant in that chamber. He gets one finger out through the crack. Does that mean he can escape through the crack? Of course not. He's too big. The only way he can get out is by breaking the chamber apart. That's what I think the steam giant is going to do any minute now.'

They watched in silence, their nerves tight. Were they far enough away? Even the doctor could not tell how strong the explosion might be. At least they were sure no natives would be hurt – their villages were on the higher part of the ridge far from the pass.

By the way, where had the villagers gone? Hal scanned the heights but could see no one around the burning houses. Falling bombs were continually starting new fires but there was no one to put them out. Where had the people disappeared to?

He looked again towards the pass. The jet of steam was now so strong and high that it looked like Old Faithful of Yellowstone. The hissing had changed to a harsh sound that cut like a knife. The giant was becoming very angry.

Then with a roar and a blast of fire he broke out of his prison, flinging rocks in all directions, cold rocks and blazing rocks and liquid lava and billowing oceans of steam that cut off the view.

Now they could see nothing – except some whizzing fragments that fell towards the deck. They dodged these to the best of their ability and waited in suspense for the cloud to clear.

It thinned with tantalizing slowness. The men strained their eyes. Now they could see the ridge again but it had changed. There was still a heavy mist where the pass should be.

As it lifted they almost choked with relief for there, shining bright between the black rocks, an open channel led from the lake to the ocean.

'Glory be!' shouted Captain Ike. 'She's all clear. Omo, engine!' He beamed at Dr Dan. 'I forgive you,' he said. 'But it's the last time you'll ever get this ship into a volcano.'

Dr Dan grinned. 'That's all right with me,' he said. 'I didn't enjoy it too much myself.'

Under power, the *Lively Lady* sailed to the pass.

'Slow,' cautioned the captain. 'May be rocks under the surface.'

The ship crept out through the channel. Her keel felt no rocks – the explosion had done its work thoroughly. In a few moments the vessel was rising and falling in the free and open ocean with all the elbow room between American and Asia. Everybody was fairly intoxicated with this new freedom.

Their gaoler roared his anger at their escape. Earthquakes shook the island, sending waves in pursuit of the *Lively Lady*, and the craters tossed out fire and showers of rocks.

Through the rumbling and the roaring came another note, a long even note, the whistle of a steamer.

'Must be the *Matua*,' said Dr Dan. 'We ought to be able to see her when we get around this headland.'

As they circled the point they could see it plainly – the approaching steamer under its plume of smoke. Hal understood now why the people had deserted the burning villages. They had seen the steamer long before and had gone down to the beach to await its coming. They stood on the shore, hundreds of brown men, women and children, and a few white men who might be Roman Catholic priests or Wesleyan missionaries. Some of the islanders had small bundles on their backs, but most had saved nothing. They stood there hopeless and homeless, their beautiful island ravaged by fire, their plantations buried under ashes and cinders, their lives endangered by the shower of death from thirty craters.

As the *Lively Lady* came near, a canoe put off from shore carrying several islanders and a white man. When it came alongside, the white man stood up in the boat and addressed Captain Ike, who was at the rail.

'My name is Kerr,' he said. 'Missionary here.'

'I'm Captain Flint. Come aboard.'

'We saw your little ship in the lake,' said Kerr as he climbed up. 'I'm afraid you had a bad night. Is there anything we could do for you now?'

Captain Ike was surprised. 'It's not a question of what you can do for us, but what we can do for you. Good of you to think of us, but you must have had a lot tougher time than we did.'

'Terrible,' admitted the missionary. 'This was one of the most beautiful islands in the South Seas. Now it's nothing but a smoking ruin. Thirteen hundred people have lost practically everything they owned. We don't know what to do – stay on the island or try to get away. It all depends on whether the eruption will die down or get worse.'

'That's something I wouldn't know,' said Captain

Ike. 'But we have a volcano man aboard – he might be able to tell you.' He introduced Dr Dan.

'I wish I could give you some encouragement,' the doctor told the missionary, 'but frankly, I believe the eruption is just starting. The worst is yet to come.'

'Then what a blessing it would be if your ship and the *Matua* could take us off. Do you think that would be possible?'

'Not only possible' said Dr Dan, 'but it's all arranged. The *Matua* is coming because I called her last night. I couldn't consult you first, and of course you don't have to leave, but I would strongly advise it. Your people have already lost what they owned – if they stay they will lose their lives as well.'

'But we can't pay for our passage.'

'That won't matter so far as the *Lively Lady* is concerned. Of course I can't speak for the skipper of the *Matua*.' Dr Dan looked at the approaching ship. 'He seems to be bearing down on us. In a few minutes he'll have a chance to speak for himself.'

The *Matua* was a big inter-island trading steamer well known in the South Seas. She was sturdily built but so old that some people claimed she dated from the days when ships of this sort carried slaves to the plantations. But whether she had ever been a slaver or not, she had broad decks and a big hold large enough to carry hundreds of passengers, provided they were willing to sleep on deck and below without bunks.

With a jingling of bells and churning of reversed propellers the *Matua* came alongside the *Lively Lady*. There it lay like a whale beside a goldfish, its bridge as high as the little ship's masthead.

From the bridge peered down a face that looked none too pleasant where it could be seen at all between the clumps of scrubby whiskers.

'You called me,' shouted the owner of the face. 'Where are the passengers?'

'Yonder on the shore,' Captain Ike replied.

'All those? Hell's bells! I've got something to do besides lug kanakas around the Pacific.'

Mr Kerr came forward. 'Captain, I'm one of the missionaries on this island. You can see what the eruption is doing to our island. The volcanologist here tells us it's going to get worse instead of better. We have to get away.'

'Oh, you have to get away, do you? So you think we have to take you. You expect us to take you away because you don't like a little fire and brimstone. What'd you come here for in the first place? You knew it was a live volcano. This ship is a trader – I have to show a profit to the owners. Now, talk business. How many people are there?'

'Thirteen hundred.'

Captain Ike said, 'We can take a hundred on the *Lively Lady*.'

'That leaves twelve hundred,' said the captain of the *Matua*. 'Where to?'

'Since the island belongs to the Queen of Tonga,' said the missionary, 'I suppose we should be taken to Tonga.'

'Tonga!' grumbled the captain. 'A good three hundred miles. Throw me two days off my schedule. Smell up my ship with twelve hundred sweating kanakas. Well, nobody can say I ain't good-hearted. I'll take the lot of you at a pound apiece.'

'Twelve hundred pounds,' muttered Hal. 'The big pirate! That's more than thirty-three hundred dollars.'

The missionary's face was flushed with anger but he kept his voice steady. 'I know this is a great inconvenience to you, captain, but it is an emergency.

You might say it's a matter of life and death. And as for your price, I have no doubt it would be fair enough under normal circumstances. But you must understand we are destitute. We would not be able to pay for our passage.'

The captain's face purpled. 'And you bring me a hundred miles off my course to tell me this? By the Holy Harry, if I had my way I'd dump you all into those craters. Goodbye – I'll see you in hell!'

He laid his hand on the telegraph to signal the engine-room.

'Wait a minute,' called Dr Dan. 'You've forgotten something. These people belong to Tonga. Perhaps the Tongan government would pay their passage.'

'Perhaps the moon is made of green cheese,' retorted the captain. 'I can't waste time on perhapses.'

'But you can easily find out,' insisted Dr Dan. 'Call Tonga and ask.'

The captain grumpily clawed his beard. Then he muttered an order to the mate who went back to the radio room.

Within twenty minutes a reply came from Tonga. Queen Salote of Tonga would personally stand responsible for the fares of the refugees.

'All right,' barked the Matua captain, 'let 'em come.'

The missionary went ashore and the people could be seen gathering around him to hear his report. Then with happy shouts they rushed to the water's edge. A few of the old folks got into the one canoe but all the rest leaped into the sea and swam for the ships, regardless of sharks. Women perched their babies on their shoulders where they could hang on to their mother's hair. The tots were not frightened for they were well used to the water. Many a Polynesian baby learns to swim before he can walk.

Up the rope ladders of the *Lively Lady* and the *Matua* clambered the dripping swimmers. Soon both ships were packed to the gunwales. Crowded together like sardines, it would be an uncomfortable voyage, but the Polynesians, with their ability to be lighthearted even in the face of disaster, chattered and laughed and sang.

(So it was that Niuafou, more often called Tin Can Island, was evacuated. The island was burned to a crisp by the frightful eruption that followed. Months later a few hardy spirits returned. Now, as this book is written, nineteen people have rebuilt their homes among the blackened ruins. There they defy the volcano god who continually mutters through his thirty mouths, 'I told them to keep off my island. Shall I have to tell them again?')

16

The Burning River

When the thirteen hundred refugees had been delivered to Her Majesty, Salote, Queen of the Tongas, the *Lively Lady* sailed for Hawaii.

All the Pacific had been talking about the eruption that for many weeks had been gathering strength on the southernmost island of the Hawaiian group.

The greatest volcano in the world, Mauna Loa, had sent lava snakes crawling down to destroy the lovely city of Hilo. Every day the fiery rivers came closer.

How could they be stopped before they reached the city?

Dr Dan was anxious to study the new eruption, and to do what he could to help solve the problem. He had another reason for wishing to land at Hawaii. There he could get rid of the *Lively Lady* and her crew.

'She's a fine little ship,' he admitted to Captain Ike as the schooner smartly tacked into the trade wind on the long 'uphill' climb to Hawaii. 'And that fellow Hal has his points – but I don't trust him.'

'You've reached the point where you don't trust anybody,' said Captain Ike. 'If you ask me, I'd say there's something wrong in your noggin.'

Dr Dan smiled in an attempt to be tolerant. 'I'm not surprised that you talk that way. Hunt has poisoned your mind against me. He's made everybody on this ship think that I'm touched in the head. For all I know, he's reported me to my bosses. He wants my job.'

'What makes you think so?'

'Why else would he invent such stories – that I lost consciousness on the edge of Asama crater – that I went wild when an earthquake struck the inn – that I got drunkenness of the deeps when we dived at

Falcon? He wants to do me in. I'm sure of it.'

'You'd have been done in several times if it hadn't been for Hal,' Captain Ike reminded him. 'Who was it that thought of using aqualungs to escape the gas? Who was it took us down into the water when we would have died of the heat? Who was it figured a way to get out when the pumice roofed us over? Who was it got my ship out of Tin Can by blowing open the pass?'

Dr Dan said no more but he was not convinced. 'Yes,' he thought to himself – 'I'm quite aware that Hunt did all those things. And that's just the trouble. I'm supposed to be the leader of this expedition – but half the time he's leading it. He's coming up with the ideas. He's as smart as he is crooked. He wants to make me look like a fool and build himself up at my expense. Well, he won't put it over. I'll fire him and all his gang the moment we set foot on Hawaii.'

But he didn't.

He was on the point of acting when they stepped ashore at Hilo. Something held him back. In some strange way, he felt that he had need of Hal.

The fiery serpents were approaching the city of Hilo and the people were in a panic. It was a difficult and dangerous situation. Ideas were needed, and Hal had a way of coming up with ideas. He would not fire Hal just yet.

There was something of nobility in his decision. He saw it to his own advantage to dismiss Hal – but to the advantage of Hilo to keep him. So he would keep him for the sake of thirty thousand terrified people who needed all the help they could find. Hal lacked technical knowledge of volcanic phenomena, but he had a way of getting people out of tight places.

So Hal and his friends could stay a little longer, just until this emergency was over. Then they must go.

Dr Dan was met on the dock by a brisk, intelligent-looking man, Dr Janno, volcanologist in charge of the volcano observatory on the slope of Mauna Loa.

'We were glad to hear you were coming,' said Dr Janno. 'Several villages have already been burned out. If something isn't done within the next two days this beautiful city will be destroyed. We need your advice.'

Dr Dan introduced Hal and Roger. Captain Ike and Omo had remained on the *Lively Lady*.

'Well, now,' said Dr Janno, 'we won't waste any time. If you'll come back to my car I'll take you up the mountain.'

Before them as they walked along the dock rose the city of Hilo in all its beauty, with its fine buildings and lovely gardens and palms. Behind it towered the giant that was threatening to stamp it out, the mighty volcano of Mauna Loa. It was so huge that it seemed about to topple over onto the city although the peak of it was really thirty-five miles away.

Roger was fascinated and a little frightened. 'Is it true,' he asked, 'that Mauna Loa is the biggest volcano on earth?'

'Quite true,' said Dr Janno. 'Not only that, but it is probably the largest single mountain of any sort on the globe. It rises 13,700 feet above sea level and goes down 18,000 feet below, so its total height is 31,700 feet. Its volume is about ten thousand cubic miles. Compare that with eighty cubic miles for Mt Shasta. Vesuvius is a child's toy compared with Mauna Loa.'

They stepped into the car, drove back through the city and up into the country. There was a continuous booming sound like the firing of heavy cannon. Frequent quakes shook the ground and opened up cracks in the road. Crews of men were working to fill the cracks so that cars could pass. But new cracks were continually opening.

One split the pavement directly ahead and the car came to a stop just in time. The crack was ten feet wide and all of fifty feet deep.

Dr Janno was not disturbed. 'We can drive around through the field,' he said, and they did so.

They were not more than half a mile out of Hilo when Dr Janno stopped the car. They got out and looked up at a huge black monster creeping along over the fields toward the city. It was thirty or forty feet high and perhaps an eighth of a mile wide. The front of it was steep like a cliff. But this was a moving cliff. It was a liquid cliff, made of yellow lava, blazing hot, steadily oozing forward towards the city.

The sides and top of the lava river were black where the lava had cooled somewhat and hardened. Every once in a while a burst of gas would explode through the black shell and break a hole through which the yellow lava could be seen. Geysers of steam shot up here and there. The whole river smoked. It made a grinding, crunching sound as it inched along.

'At the rate it is moving,' said Dr Janno, 'it will reach Hilo in two days.'

The yellow front of the river touched a group of trees and they went up in flames as if they had been made of paper. Behind the trees was a house. Its family had deserted it and it stood there looking small and terrified in the path of the fiery colossus. A yellow finger reached out and touched the house. It seemed to explode rather than burn and in a few minutes it had completely disappeared in smoke.

'You can see what is going to happen when the lava flow reaches the city,' Dr Janno said. 'Well, come along. I have more to show you.'

They drove on over broken and patched roads, steadily climbing the mountain slope. They stopped at last on the brink of a crater. They looked down into a pit six hundred feet deep to a lake of boiling lava.

'This is Kilauea,' Dr Janno said. 'Anywhere else on earth it would be called a great volcano. But here it plays second fiddle to Mauna Loa. See that hotel on the edge of the crater? It's entirely heated by steam from the volcano.'

They drove several thousand feet higher, then left the car and walked. They came again to the river of lava. Here, too, it was more than thirty feet high but only about a hundred feet wide. And now they could see where it all came from. It did not issue from the crater of Mauna Loa but from a fissure on the slope. It came out in tremendous spurts and fountains, shooting five hundred feet high, a sight to take the breath away. The sound was like the roar of a great waterfall. The liquid rock fell all about the crack and then flowed down the mountainside. For several hundred yards it kept its yellow colour. Then it darkened as the outside was cooled by the mountain air. A little further down the outside crust was black and stiff. But the river of fire flowed on inside it.

'That is the way our lava tunnels are formed,' Dr Janno said. 'If the fountain should suddenly stop all the lava in the tunnel would keep on flowing until it had come out the lower end. Then you would have a hollow tunnel. We have one twenty-seven miles long on this island, and another six miles long. People sometimes make their homes inside these tunnels, and thieves use them as their hide-out.'

Roger was fascinated by the five-hundred foot geysers of fire.

'They look like devils dancing,' he said.

Dr Janno laughed. 'That's what the Hawaiians think, but they regard them as goddesses, not devils. Let me tell you a little of the story of this volcano – it's rather thrilling. The chief goddess in charge is Pele –

when the craters erupt the natives say that Pele and her sisters are dancing, and they will dance down the mountainside and kill the people unless something is done to please them. Pele is supposed to be fond of pigs and ohelo berries, so these are tossed into the flames as offerings.

'Once, in the year 1790, an army camped near by and failed to make offerings to Pele. There was a frightful eruption and four hundred people were killed.

'When new eruptions came eleven years later the priests tried to satisfy the goddesses by throwing live hogs into the burning stream, but it did no good. Finally, the great King Kamehameha cut off his own hair and gave it as an offering. Pele was apparently satisfied and the lava ceased to flow.

'But a few years later Pele was once more making mischief. The people begged the royal lady Kapiolani to make offerings to the angry goddess. But she had been to school and had no use for the old superstitions. She walked to the edge of Kilauea crater, broke off a branch of berries from an ohelo tree and, instead of throwing half of them in to Pele as was the custom, she ate them all. The people trembled and waited for her to be struck down by a shaft of fire, but she was not harmed.

'You would have thought that that would kill the superstition for good and all. But it did not. In 1880 a great lava flow came dangerously close to Hilo and the people begged Princess Ruth to save them. She went to the river of fire, made a prayer to Pele, then tossed in a bottle of brandy and six red silk handkerchiefs. The flow stopped at the very edge of the town.

'Of course that revived the old superstition. When there was another eruption in 1887 the native priests said it could be satisfied only by the sacrifice of a victim of royal blood. The Princess Likelike starved herself to death to appease the anger of Pele. That time it didn't work – Pele went right on making trouble.

'You would think the Hawaiians would have grown out of such a notion by this time but, believe it or not, many of the natives are throwing pigs and ohelo berries into this river in an attempt to stop it before it reaches their homes. They pray to Pele – then they go to the churches and pray to the Christian God.'

Dr Dan said, 'With their homes in danger, they must feel desperate. You can hardly blame them for trying everything.'

'It's human nature,' agreed Dr Janno. 'But if their prayers are going to be answered I'm afraid it is we volcano men who will have to do something about it. It's our job – but I've racked my brain and can't think of any way to stop that flow before it reaches Hilo.'

It was a magnificent and terrible sight, the great river, yellow near its source, black lower down, zigzagging around hills and through ravines, down thirty-five miles of mountain slope to within half a mile of the city.

About a thousand feet below where they stood the river bent sharply to the right to get past a rocky knoll.

'Down there where it turns right,' Hal said. 'What would happen if it could be made to turn left instead?'

Dr Janno was amused. 'That is what President Roosevelt used to call an iffy question,' he said. 'There's not much point in thinking about it since no power on earth could turn that river out of its course.'

'But if it could be done . . .' persisted Hal.

'Oh, if it could be done, of course our problem

would be solved. The flow would follow that ravine to the northeast.'

'Would it strike any village or town?'

'No. There is nothing but wild country down that valley.'

'So it could flow down and into the sea without doing any harm?'

'Yes. But as I said, it can't be done.'

'Perhaps not,' said Hal. 'But I was just wondering – if the river could be dammed at that point so that it would flow the other way . . .'

'My dear young man,' said Dr Janno impatiently, 'how could you possibly dam that stream? It has about the volume of Niagara below the Falls. In fact, the Niagara River would be much easier to dam because it flows out in the open. This one is flowing inside a rock tunnel. How could you get at it to dam it?'

Dr Dan saw that Janno was irritated. 'Forget it, Hal,' he said. 'We mustn't waste Dr Janno's time with impossible schemes. We've got to be practical.'

But Hal was not willing to give up yet. 'You said no power on earth could stop it,' he said. 'I believe you are right.'

'Well, I'm glad you see that,' said Dr Janno.

'Perhaps no power on earth could do it,' went on Hal, 'but how about sky power? Couldn't planes drop bombs? Or am I being too imaginative?'

'I think you are,' said Dr Janno, and he turned to Dr Dan. 'I wonder if we could continue our discussion without further interruptions from your young friend?'

Hal grinned. 'Sorry, doctor. I know when I'm not wanted,' and he wandered down the slope to take a closer look at the bend in the river.

17
Bombs to Save Lives

'A most persistent young man!' said Dr Janno.

But Dr Dan did not answer. He was gazing thoughtfully at the black river. 'It's just possible,' he mused.

'Now, doctor,' said Janno, 'you're not giving any serious thought . . .'

'Yes, I think it's worth considering. That crust over the lava flow – how thick do you suppose it is?'

'Oh, I don't know, perhaps six feet – perhaps ten.'

'Would a demolition bomb break it up?'

'That's a question that only a bomb expert could answer. I suppose if they used enough bombs they could smash the roof.'

'Then the broken pieces would fall into the stream. If there were enough of them they would dam it up and make it overflow in the other direction.'

'Pretty theoretical,' objected Dr Janno. 'Besides, where would you get the bombers?'

'What's the matter with the U.S. Army? Isn't there a bombing squadron stationed at Luke Field?'

'I believe so. But they wouldn't touch it. Their job is war, nor volcanoes. This would be an expensive operation. They wouldn't feel justified in spending military money on a civilian project.'

'I seem to remember,' said Dr Dan, 'that army planes have sometimes been used during national disasters, such as fires and floods. As for expense, it wouldn't be as costly as the loss of the city of Hilo. What do you say we ask them?'

'I don't understand,' said Dr Janno, 'why you give so much weight to the wild suggestion of a boy who has been reading too much science fiction. He seems to have considerable influence over you.'

Dr Dan reddened with anger and embarrassment. 'I don't care to discuss that. My relations with Hunt are not as pleasant as you suppose. In fact, he's about to be dismissed. All the same, I feel this notion of his is worth looking into. After all, it won't do any harm to ask.'

Dr Janno waved his hands in grudging consent. 'Very well, we'll ask. We'll go down to the observatory and telephone.'

They called Hal and returned to the car. They drove back to the edge of Kilauea crater and entered the Volcano Observatory. It was a stone building built to resist the falling fires of the volcano. It was full of fascinating machines, the magnetometer, seismograph, pyrometers, gravimeters, spectroscopes, and the walls were covered with charts and diagrams. Dr Janno took up the phone and called Major Hugh C. Gilchrist, commander of the Kilauea Military Camp. He explained Hal's proposal to the major.

'Please understand,' he said, 'that this is not my suggestion. Personally, I consider it totally impractical. I doubt that any bombing squadron could deliver enough power to turn the flow from its course.'

The others could not hear the major's answer. Then Janno spoke again. 'Oh, you misunderstood me. I didn't mean to imply that the Army can't do great things with its demolition bombs. But you must realize that you are dealing here with one of the greatest forces of nature.'

Another pause. Then Janno again: 'Well, I'm surprised that you take the suggestion seriously. Remember, I do not stand responsible for it. However, if you wish to call Honolulu . . .'

He put down the phone. His eyes were wide open with astonishment as he turned to face Dr Dan and the boys. 'The major thinks it's worth a try,' he said. 'He's going to radio the Chief of Staff in Honolulu. We're to wait here for further word.'

In half an hour the major called back to say that a plane with three officers of the bombing squadron on board was on the way to inspect the lava flow area. The volcanologists were requested to go back to the bend to mark by their presence the exact spot where the bombing should take place.

They returned at once to the right-angle kink in the tunnel of fire. The flight from Honolulu would take about an hour. While waiting, they carefully inspected the terrain. Dr Janno became more optimistic.

The plane came in over Hilo and followed the lava stream up the mountain to the point where the men stood. There it circled round and round while the bombing officers studied the situation, made measurements, and took photographs. Then the plane flew off in the direction of Honolulu.

The volcano men returned to the observatory and anxiously waited for a report. Hal could hardly bear the suspense. When he closed his eyes in an effort to keep calm, he could only see the fiery claws of the orange-and-black monster that, given two days more, would wipe out the homes of thirty thousand people.

The answer came at last, but not over the phone. Major Gilchrist arrived in person. He was fairly bursting with news.

'They are going to do it,' he said. 'The Army Transport *Royal T. Frank* is already on the way with twenty six-hundred-pound TNT bombs and twenty three-hundred-pound pointer bombs. The ship will get here early tomorrow morning. The bombing planes will be scheduled to arrive at the same time, ten of them. The Ordnance Department will supply several civilian employees to supervise unloading the bombs from the ship, fusing them, and loading them into the planes. Then we'll take a crack at your river.'

Dr Janno warned him, 'That may be all you can do – crack it.'

'We'll do better than that. You'd be surprised to see what a mess a six-hundred-pounder can make. The bomb men tell me it will dig a hole twelve feet deep in solid rock. It ought to smash up the crust on top of that flow.'

'I'm rather surprised,' said Dr Janno, 'that the Army is so much interested.'

'Why shouldn't we be interested? Hilo is the

second largest city in the Hawaiian Islands. Naturally we want to save it if we can. And it isn't only the city. Hilo Harbour is second only to Pearl Harbour and very important from the standpoint of defence. If this flow continues it will not only destroy the city but fill the harbour. So you see we have good military reasons, as well as humanitarian reasons, for doing what we can to stop it.'

18
Forest Fire

Early the next morning the ship arrived and the bombs were transferred to the airfield where ten fighter-bombers, two observation planes and two amphibians were already waiting. They had come in at dawn from Luke Field, Honolulu, and were manned by twenty officers and thirty-seven men.

Each plane was loaded with two six-hundred-pound demolition bombs, armed with 0.1 second delayed action fuse, and two three-hundred-pound practice bombs for sighting shots. The first attack-bomber took off at 8.45 a.m. and was followed by the others at twenty-minute intervals.

The two observation planes flew to the point where the bombing was to take place and circled to watch the operation. The officers had invited Dr Janno and Dr Dan to accompany them in one observation plane, and Hal and Roger in the other. The boys looked down with the greatest interest at the bend in the black snake as the first bombing plane came over.

A black object dropped from the plane. It struck the

rock roof of the river just at the bend and sent up a grey ball of smoke. It did not seem to have damaged the roof.

'That was just one of the three-hundred-pound practice bombs,' said the officer beside Hal. 'It contains only black powder and sand so it will send up a cloud of smoke that can be plainly seen. Then the bombers can tell whether they are on the target.'

The fighter-bomber circled and came back over the bend. It climbed high, poised, pitched forward, and dropped another black object, much larger this time. This was one of the six-hundred-pound TNT bombs.

It struck and exploded with a sound like a crash of thunder. The surface of the lava stream that had cooled and hardened into black rock was split into thousands of fragments that flew in all directions. The explosion had broken through the roof and a fountain of white-hot lava from the flowing river beneath shot up into the sky several hundred feet. There it turned to orange-red, glistened in the sun, spread out like a fan, and fell again. The black serpent had lost some of his life-blood. The officers were delighted with the result.

The plane came in again and dropped another big bomb. This one broke a hole twenty or thirty feet wide and the great broken chunks of black rock fell into the lava river, partially choking it. Lava began to overflow from the hole and run off to the left.

This was just what Hal had hoped for. He was greatly elated, but he reminded himself that there is many a slip, and something might go wrong yet. He waited eagerly for the next bomber.

This one dropped a practice bomb but it went sadly off target. It came in and dropped another exactly on the bend. It circled again and this time let go a big fellow. This one enlarged the hole in the roof by twenty feet, and the lava crust, broken up into boulders, tumbled into the stream. The dam was building up higher. The second bomb added to the obstruction and increased the overflow. This had now formed a definite stream of glowing lava, as yet only six or seven feet wide, running off in the opposite direction into the valley that would carry it harmless to the sea.

Every bomb continued the damage until the monster's back was completely broken and the opening filled with rock. The choked river, seeking a way of escape, poured out at the side and down in a mighty river through the uninhabited valley.

Hilo was saved. The liquid lava in the tube below the dam would continue for a while to ooze out at the lower end but would spread and harden before it could reach the town.

Hal's satisfaction was marred by a new anxiety. He noticed that the orange-red river in its new course down the wild valley was threatening at one point to climb over a ridge. On the other side of this ridge was a little settlement of a few houses that would be burned out if the river succeeded in reaching them.

When the bombing mission was completed and the observation planes had returned to the airfield, Hal mentioned what he had seen to Dr Janno and Dr Dan.

'Yes, I noticed that,' said Dr Janno. 'No use talking

with the army men about it – it's not a job for bombing planes. But I do think we ought to drive up there and investigate it. Unfortunately I have to get back to the observatory.'

'Then suppose we investigate for you,' proposed Dr Dan.

'Good. But you'll need a car. I think I can borrow an army jeep for you.'

In the borrowed jeep, Dr Dan, Hal and Roger drove northwest over a low range of hills, then west up the wild valley through which the new lava flow was crawling to meet them. The little-used road was really nothing more than a trail and made rough riding. Finally, they got to the ridge where they could see the settlement on one side and the lava river on the other.

'It doesn't look so bad from here,' said Dr Dan. 'The ridge is high enough to protect the village. I think we can report that all's well.' He looked at the approaching river. 'It's coming fast. Let's get out of here.'

They backed the jeep around and drove down again into the wild valley. The air was very hot. Smoke and steam drifted overhead, and curious strings of glassy thread. These accumulated on the bushes until they were loaded with them like decorated Christmas trees.

'What are all those stringy things?' Roger wanted to know.

'It's lava,' said Dr Dan. 'The superstitious natives call it Pele's Hair. They say that the furious goddess is tearing her hair and casting it out on the winds. Actually it comes from the fountains of lava that spurt up from the river. The wind tears this sticky stuff apart and pulls it out into long threads and blows it all over the country to decorate the trees and bushes.'

The forest was high around them now and they could see the molten river. They should be getting farther from it – but, strangely enough, the heat seemed to be increasing. There was the crackling sound of burning trees.

Then they came around a turn to find the road blocked by a stream of blazing lava ten feet high. They brought the jeep to a sudden halt.

'No chance of going that way,' said Dr Dean. 'We'll have to go back and see where this trail leads.'

About they went and back up the trail.

The increasing smoke made them cough. The bushes were burning now at the side of the road. The heat was intense.

Suddenly the jeep again came to a halt, facing another yellow stream.

Evidently the river had divided into two flows and they were neatly caught between them. Every tree or bush the lava touched burst into flame. The fire was licking the wheels of the jeep.

'Let's get out of this thing before it blows up,' said Hal, and they tumbled out.

They plunged into the woods with the fire close behind them. It was a tropical forest, full of logs and tangled with vines, and they had no machetes. They tore at the brambles and creepers and scratched their way through.

They gasped and panted and fought and moved forward – but the fire was coming forward, too, and its fiery breath scorched their backs. Side by side, tense, terrified, they slashed their way through the jungle. Their arms ached, their hands bled. The fire was gaining on them. The burning of their legs, backs and the nape of their necks was hard to bear and they could smell their own scorched hair.

Roger, the smallest, could wriggle through faster. He was some ten yards ahead. Hal came next with Dr Dan crashing along behind him. Suddenly this noise stopped and Hal looked around to see what had happened to Dr Dan.

The doctor was no longer fighting. He was standing as rigid as a monument. Then his muscles suddenly let go and he crumpled in a heap on the ground.

'Roger!' Hal called. 'The Doctor!'

They picked up the limp form of the scientist and struggled with it through the bush. Foot by foot they advanced and second by second the heat increased and all around them the leaves were shrivelling and crackling into fire.

At last they burst through jumbled-up branches into an open stretch of gravelled ground. Breathless and choking, drenched with sweat, they carried their burden on down the valley. Behind them the wall of forest they had just left went up in flames with a great crackling roar.

There was another sound now, the drone of a motor, and an army jeep came rattling up the valley to stop beside them.

'It looked pretty bad over here,' said the driver. 'We thought you might need help. Climb in.'

Thankfully they loaded the still unconscious doctor into the car and got in after him.

'What happened to your buddy?' said the officer at the wheel.

'Went blank and won't come out of it,' Hal said. 'I'm afraid it's not just an ordinary faint. Something basic. I think we'd better get him to the hospital right away.'

'There's a place in Hilo,' said the officer. 'But I think if it's anything serious we'd better get him to Queen's Hospital in Honolulu. It's only five minutes more to the airfield and we'll commandeer a plane for you. Within an hour he'll be in bed.'

Grateful for an army that can do more than fight, Hal and Roger saw the doctor transferred to an army plane and they flew with him to Honolulu. The hospital, notified by radio telephone, had an ambulance at the airfield to meet them and soon the unconscious scientist was under a physician's care in the famous Queen's Hospital.

He lay with eyes wide open staring fixedly at the ceiling. His breathing was rapid and his pulse fast. He evidently knew nothing whatever of what was going on. Hal and Roger sat near while the physician, Dr James Clark, made his examination. Then the doctor sat down and faced Hal.

'Tell me, how did this happen?'

'We were working our way through the brush to

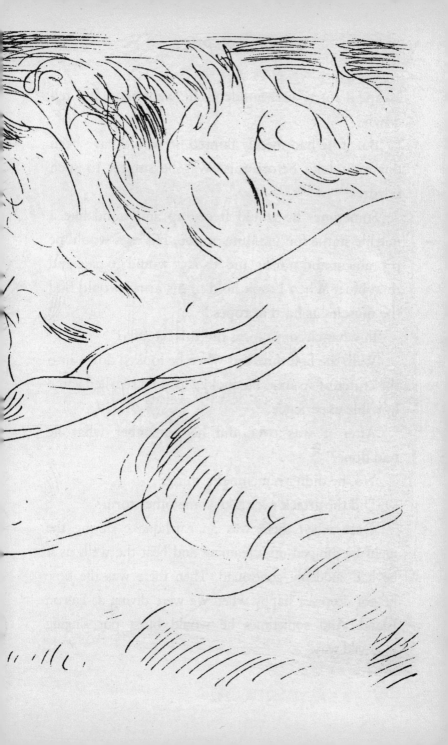

escape a forest fire. Suddenly he went rigid and fell down.'

'But if he had merely fainted he would have been out of it long before this. Was he subject to such seizures?'

'Sometimes he would freeze up and stand like a marble statue for a minute or two. His eyes would be prominent and staring and his face would go pale and then blue. When I took hold of his arm I would find the muscles as hard as ropes.'

'In what circumstances did this happen?'

'Well, the first time was when he looked down into the crater of Asama. He looked as if he recalled some horrible experience.'

'After it was over, did he remember what he had done?'

'No, he didn't remember a thing.'

'Did the attack ever take some other form?'

'Once when there was an earthquake during the night he jumped up screaming and beat the walls as if he had suddenly gone mad. Then there was the time he got deep-sea happy when we were diving at Falcon Island. And sometimes he would burst out singing in a wild way.'

'Very interesting,' said Dr Clark. 'I'm beginning to see a pattern. How about his disposition – was he sometimes irritable?'

'He became very suspicious. He thought we were all conspiring against him.'

'Exactly,' said Dr Clark. 'It sounds very much like *petit mal*.'

'What's that?' asked Roger curiously.

'Well, it's a mild form of epilepsy.'

Hal was startled. 'I never thought of that. I always supposed an epileptic was – well – weak in the head, a bit insane. But Dr Adams is a very intelligent man, even brilliant.'

'My friend,' said Dr Clark, 'don't forget that we are all weak in the head and a bit insane. And as for epileptics, some of them have been men of unusual mental ability. Julius Caesar, Petrarch, Peter the Great, Mohammed, Napoleon – every one of them an epileptic, and a genius. Some forms of epilepsy are very terrible. Since you don't say anything about convulsions, I assume that this is the mild form, *petit mal*. Don't be deceived by the word mild. It is mild compared with the extreme form called *grand mal*, but even *petit mal* can be fatal.'

'But what could have been the cause of it?'

'There are many possible causes. Mental shock could do it, or a physical injury. In his line of work, I would guess that some time he might have had a nerve-racking experience, or an accident, or both.'

'He once began to tell our captain about some terrible experience he had had, but then stopped. He evidently didn't want to talk about it.'

'Did he ever complain of chronic pain in any part of his body?'

'Nothing but a headache in his left temple. He didn't seem to attach much importance to it.'

'Ah, but it may be very important. I think we'll take an X-ray of that head.'

The patient was still unconscious when brought back from the X-ray room. The physician closeted himself with two other doctors and together they went over the negatives. Then Dr Clark returned to Hal, still carrying the pictures. He held one up to the light.

'There's the cause of the trouble,' he said. 'That dark wedge – it's an internally broken piece of the skull and it presses upon a nerve centre. At some time or other he has suffered a blow on the head as well as severe psychological shock. That wedge must come out and it is important that the operation be performed at once or he may never regain consciousness. Can we get the consent of his nearest of kin?'

'I don't know anything about them,' said Hal. 'He's employed by the American Museum of Natural History in New York. They would know.'

'We'll cable them at once. But there's no time to be lost. While we're waiting for a reply we'll go ahead with preparations just as if we were sure the answer would be yes.'

Dr Dan was already on the operating table and the surgeon standing by when consent came from the scientist's father in New York. The operation proceeded at once.

In the corridor outside the operating room was a row of chairs for anxious friends – 'worry row' as Roger called it. He and Hal waited there for word from within. They realized now how fond they had become of the young scientist, in spite of his sick suspicions. Brain surgery was a delicate and dangerous business. The patient, already weakened by shock, might pass out under the strain.

Half an hour, and still no word. Then a nurse came

out of the operating room and scurried down the hall. Hal was after her in a flash. 'How's it going?' The girl shook her head and hurried on.

Hal went back and sat down heavily in his chair. Now what did that shake of the head mean? That the nurse wasn't allowed to talk – or that the worst had happened?

A full hour went by. The boys were out of their chairs now and pacing up and down the corridor, as anxious as expectant fathers.

Then the operating room door opened and a body covered by a white sheet was wheeled out and down the hall. The boys waited impatiently for the doctors. At last Dr Clark and the surgeon came out and hurried past.

'Wait a minute!' demanded Hal, and the physician turned back.

'Is he all right?'

'He'll do,' the doctor said. 'The operation was successful. We got the wedge out but of course the whole area is inflamed. Your friend will need a long rest – six months or so before he goes poking into any more volcanoes. Now, if you'll excuse me . . .' and he was off.

With mixed feelings Hal and Roger walked back to

their patient's room. Their chief feeling was of relief that the operation had been a success. But they were unhappy to learn that their volcano expedition was ended.

Again they sat beside Dr Dan's bed. He was still unconscious, but it was different now, and better. The staring eyes had closed and the breathing was slower and relaxed.

'Just a good, normal sleep,' the doctor said. 'Why don't you boys go and get something to eat?'

Roger went out while Hal stayed beside the patient. When Roger returned Hal set forth, but as he passed the reception desk on the main floor he heard a man asking for Dr Dan Adams.

Hal stopped. 'I heard you inquiring for Dr Adams,' he said.

'Yes. I'm a reporter for the *Honolulu Advertiser*. I wanted to interview him about the bombing.'

'Sorry, he's in no shape to be interviewed. He's just had an operation and now he's asleep.'

'Could you be his assistant, Hal Hunt?'

'That's right.'

'Then perhaps you could give me the story.'

Hal hesitated. 'I'd rather he'd do it – but I don't

know when he'll be able to. Very well, I'll tell you what I can.'

Hal had hardly finished with the reporter when two more men came inquiring for Dr Adams. The reception clerk told them he could not be seen and they were just turning away when Hal introduced himself.

'I'm Dr Adams's assistant,' he said. 'Can I do anything for you?'

'This is Mr Sinclair and my name is Scott. Like Dr Adams, we work for the American Museum. The museum has just cabled us that Adams is in this hospital and we came to see if there is anything we can do.'

'That's very good of you,' said Hal. 'He's asleep now, and I was just going out to get a bite to eat. Perhaps you'll join me and we can talk about it in the restaurant.'

Over pancakes and bacon with coconut cream and coffee, Hal told the scientists of the stirring events of that day – the bombing of the lava flow, the escape from the forest fire, the flight to Honolulu, and the operation. 'The doctor says he'll have to take six months' rest.'

'Where does that leave you?' said Sinclair.

'At a loose end, I guess,' said Hal. 'But it doesn't matter about us. The important thing is for him to get well. You haven't told me what sort of work you are doing for the museum.'

'It's an interesting job,' said Sinclair. 'They are trying to collect some information about whales and whaling. It's easy enough to learn about modern whaling methods – what they want to know is how whaling was done in the exciting days of sailing ships and whaleboats. There are just a few of those famous old ships still on the seas. We've discovered one that still goes after whales and we're going to go with her.'

Hal's eyes sparkled. 'You are in for some fun,' he said. 'I'd like to hear more about that – but just now I want to get back to our patient. How about dropping around again tomorrow morning? He may be awake then and able to see you.'

Dr Dan slept all the rest of the day and all night. The boys would have liked to stay by him but hospital rules did not permit it. They went to a hotel and came back in the morning.

19
Understanding

Dr Clark met them in the lower hall. 'Your man is awake,' he said, 'and anxious to see you. I think you will find him much changed.'

The nurse let them into the room. Dr Dan lay with eyes closed and in his hand was a copy of the morning paper.

'You won't stay too long, please,' the nurse warned. 'He's still quite weak, you know.'

'Weak, nothing,' said Dr Dan, opening his eyes – and the boys noticed that there was none of that bright hardness in his look to which they had become so unpleasantly accustomed. 'I feel like a new man. Everything looks different to me this morning. Boys, sit down, I have something to say to you. It's in the nature of an apology.'

'That isn't necessary,' Hal said. 'Wouldn't you do better just to lie quietly and let us talk?'

'No, I must tell you this. I've been very unfair to both of you, and to Captain Ike and Omo, too. I wish they were here so I could tell them so.'

'They'll be coming,' said Hal. 'I sent them a telegram last night.'

'The doctor has been telling me a lot of things I didn't know,' went on Dr Dan. 'He says I haven't been normal for a long time. And I can see now that he is right. I've been a perfect stinker, but I hope you won't blame it on me but on that wedge in my head. He tells me I've been having lapses of memory and any one of them could have done me in if you hadn't been there to look after me.' He reached out and gripped Hal's hand, and Roger's. 'And all the time I thought . . . I'm very much ashamed of what I thought. Especially when I saw your interview. Of course you've seen it.'

'No, we didn't stop to get a paper.'

Hal took up the newspaper. The whole first page was devoted to the story of the bombing of the lava flow. There were pictures of the explosions, photographed from the observation planes. There was a statement by Dr Janno, and an expression of gratitude from the mayor of Hilo. There were reports by the bombardment officers and a general military report by the Chief of Staff who stated:

'The total cost to the army of this operation was

$25,000. It saved from destruction buildings and property worth at least $51,000,000. Therefore from a purely financial standpoint the operation appears to have been justified. More important was the saving of the lives and homes of thirty thousand people. Those who witnessed the bombing declare that the execution of the mission was superb and that the bombs were placed exactly where they should have been. This aerial bombing of a lava flow made history for science in performing a great geological experiment with success.'

Then there was the interview with Hal, one paragraph of which ran as follows:

'In spite of Dr Janno's statement that the bombing was originally the idea of Mr Hal Hunt, Mr Hunt, when interviewed, refused to accept the credit. He attributed the success of the operation to the careful and brilliant plans laid by the visiting volcanologist, Dr Dan Adams.'

'I felt pretty cheap when I read that,' said Dr Dan. 'And after all my crazy notions that you were out to discredit me and take my job. I can't understand now how I ever got such ideas. Of course the bombing plan was yours, and you're going to be stuck with it as soon as I'm able to talk to reporters. They're going to get the real story.'

'Don't bother about that,' said Hal. 'Your job now is to take a good long rest and get well. Then there'll be some more volcanoes to be conquered.'

'And I'll be ready for them! I won't be afraid any more. I'm not afraid now.'

'Afraid!' said Roger. 'I never noticed that you were afraid.'

'I'm glad I was able to conceal it. Every time we came near an eruption I was all nerves, ready to jump out of my skin. It all began . . .'

He stopped, and smiled. 'I never wanted to talk about it. It was one of those horrible things you want to forget. Now I don't care whether I remember it or not. It was at the volcano Paricutin in Mexico. I slipped and fell several hundred feet down the inside slope of the crater and gave my head an awful whack on a rock. It knocked me unconscious, and when I did come to I found the slope was too steep to climb. I was roasted by the heat from the boiling lava and weak and giddy from the blow on my head. I spent all night in that crater and every hour worse things happened in my head. It was like torture in the dungeons of the Inquisition. Every moment it seemed I couldn't stand it an instant longer. Then I had my first lapse of memory and during it I got out of there, I can never tell how. But ever since then I have had a deadly fear of volcanoes. Now, thanks to the operation, my fear is gone. After a few months I'll go back to volcanoes and they'll be just a job to me, like any other. But that's enough about me – how about you? I'm afraid I'm leaving you rather up in the air.'

'Honolulu is a busy place,' Hal said. 'We'll probably find something to do here.'

'Well, I have a suggestion. Before you came this morning I had a short call from two of my colleagues at the American Museum. I believe you met them yesterday – Sinclair and Scott.'

'Yes, I talked with them,' Hal said. 'Their project sounds pretty exciting.'

'They liked you,' Dr Dan said. 'And what I told them about you and Roger didn't make them like you any the less. They're looking for some young fellows to help them on their whaling expedition. How would it appeal to you?'

Roger's eyes began to pop with excitement.

'After all,' went on Dr Dan, 'you'd still be working

for the American Museum. Just a change of bosses.'

'We don't want a change of bosses,' Hal said. 'We'd rather go on with you. But since we can't – the whaling sounds great. We'll think about it. Now we're leaving so you can have some rest.'

'Well, don't think about it too long. They're leaving in a few days.'

The boys walked down the hall, strange emotions churning in their chests.

'What a chance!' exclaimed Roger. 'A few days to decide! A few minutes is enough for me.'

But Hal, as the older and wiser, felt that the matter must not be decided hastily. In fact, he did not make up his mind until they were out of the front door.

WILLARD PRICE

Willard Price was born in 1887 in Peterborough, Ontario. He had a special interest in natural history, ethnology and exploration and made numerous expeditions for the American Museum of Natural History and the National Geographic Society.

He went on to edit various magazines on travel and world affairs and spent six years working in Japan as foreign correspondent for New York and London newspapers. He wrote fourteen adventure stories featuring Hal and Roger Hunt. He died in 1983.